Goddess Girls

IRIS THE COLORFUL

JOAN HOLUB & SUZANNE WILLIAMS

Aladdin

NEW YORK LONDON TORONTO SYDNEY NEW DELHI

ALADDIN
An imprint of Simon & Schuster Children's Publishing Division
1230 Avenue of the Americas, New York, New York 10020
First Aladdin hardcover edition August 2014

Also available in an Aladdin paperback edition.

Designed by Karin Paprocki
The text of this book was set in Baskerville Handcut.
Manufactured in the United States of America 1014 FFG
2 4 6 8 10 9 7 5 3
Library of Congress Control Number 2014940500
ISBN 978-1-4424-8824-3 (hc)
ISBN 978-1-4424-8823-6 (pbk)
ISBN 978-1-4424-8825-0 (eBook)

CONTENTS

We appreciate our mega-amazing readers!

Sabrina E. & Sophia E., Emma H., McKay O. & Reese O., Jaden B., Taelyne C., Madison M., Isabella K., Cassandra B., Michelle J., Rachel D., Olivia H., Sarah S., Laura N., Scout L. & Sofia W., Olivia S., Sara S., Megan D., Charlotte D., Kaylee S., Nani P., Carly P., Jenny C., Claire K., Lorelai M., Karis C., Brianna W., Jaimie AK., Sofía G., Hailey M., Mackenzie Z., Emma J., Ariel C., Eden O., Ella S., Lea S., Kayla S., Madison W., Sidney G., Tiffany N., Madison W., Anna F., Michela P., Caitlin R., Abby G., Malerie G. & Haylie G., Amanda W., Amanda S., Sabrina S., Liana, Hope F., Jiana B., Rachel U., Meghan B., Taylor H., Ashley C., The Andrade Family & Alba C., Yesenia O., Raven G., Alexandra E.S., Jennifer T., Sydney G., Hailey G., Emily M., Michelle S., Khanya S., Christine D-H., Karinna L., Kylie L., Micaila S., Justine Y.; Jessie F., Christine F., Melissa G., Sarah S., Sabrina P., Michaela P., Anh H., Hatsune M., Khayra H., Tawney K., Vivian Z., Gracie D., Ryanna L., April L., Izabel K., Prisca M., Lily-Ann S., Emily B., Erin K., Valerie L., Stephanie V., Melanie C., Adara R., Jennifer R., Katie M., Laura D.P., and you!

–J.H. and S.W.

Goddess Girls

IRIS THE COLORFUL

1

Rainbows

"IT'S RAINBOW TIME!" IRIS ANNOUNCED. SHE narrowed her lavender eyes and drew her arm way back as though she were going to throw a spear.

Her BFF, Antheia, the goddess of flowering wreaths, turned to watch the sky expectantly. Both goddessgirls were standing out on the Mount Olympus Academy sports fields on a beautiful, happy Sunday.

Brrrng! There was a sound like the strum of a harp

as Iris hurled what she held in her hand toward the sky. But what she threw wasn't a spear. It was a streaming, gleaming ball of magic! It left her fingers, trailing long flowy ribbons of iridescent colors. When it reached the sky, it curled, looped, and blossomed into a big bouquet of brightly hued flowers all made of light.

Other Academy students on the fields looked up, pointed, and smiled at her creation. Antheia jumped up and down, clapping in delight. Her bouncing made the cute wreath of ferns and berries that encircled her straight brown hair like a crown tilt sideways. "That was amazing! Do some more," she urged as she straightened her wreath.

"Okay." Iris was tickled pink at her friend's enthusiasm. Literally. Her hair was actually turning various shades of pink, from coral to bubble gum to fuchsia. It often did that, changing color to match her outfit, her mood, or just because. In fact, as she looked around the sports fields now for inspiration, her hair slowly shifted through all the colors of the rainbow, from red to orange to yellow, green, blue, indigo, violet, and soft shades of all the colors in between.

"Hmm. What should I make?" she murmured, tucking her long wavy hair behind her ears. A light breeze had begun to blow across the fields, and the small sparkly pink wings at Iris's back fluttered gently.

Just then her gaze fell on the four members of the Goddessgirls Cheer Squad practicing over by the bleachers. Athena, Persephone, Aphrodite, and Artemis were apparently working on new cheers. Many immortal students went to the Academy—all of them beautiful, handsome, powerful, and awesome, with softly glittering skin. But these four girls were the most popular of all the goddessgirls at MOA.

Athena was the goddess of wisdom and inventions, among other things; Persephone was the goddess of flowers; Aphrodite was the goddess of love and beauty; and Artemis—a skilled archer—was the goddess of the hunt. And Iris's BFF, of course, was the goddess of flowering wreaths.

Lucky them! Seemed like almost all the immortal MOA students were the goddesses or gods of something. However, even though Iris was a goddess, too, she wasn't officially the goddess of anything special. Which was *so* majorly lame. She loved rainbows and was good at making them. If only Principal Zeus would recognize her special skill and name her the official goddess of rainbows!

Well, somehow she was going to make that happen. And that was the reason she'd come out to the fields to practice creating different-shaped rainbows this morning.

Iris wound up again, then threw. *Brrrng!* Another ball of magic left her fingers. Streaming colored ribbons of light, it sailed in a high arc overhead to form three huge, gleaming blue-and-gold letters: *MOA*. Blue-and-gold pom-poms that actually shook appeared around the letters.

Aphrodite was the first to notice the colorful letters and pom-poms and pointed them out to her three Cheer Squad besties. All four girls smiled and waved to Iris in thanks.

"You're getting better at this," Antheia told Iris. "If you ever get a chance to show Principal Zeus what you can do, he's going to be impressed. I just know it!"

"You think?" Iris said uncertainly. "I wish I could make my rainbows do something *really* amazing to show him, though. I mean, they're pretty and all. But to gain Zeus's notice maybe they need to do something worthwhile and practical, too. Something that'll prove I deserve to be Goddess of Rainbows. Like your wreaths—they're pretty *and* useful, since they're worn during ceremonies and used as prizes in the Olympic Games."

"Could you get your rainbows to make music? Or fight enemies?" Antheia suggested.

Iris cocked her head. "Actually, I was thinking of using them as transportation. Like a long smooth slide to nearby and faraway places. Wouldn't that be fun?"

"Yes!" said Antheia, her eyes rounding at the exciting notion. "It'd be awesome. But can you make them strong enough and long enough for riding?"

"I'm working on it."

The Goddessgirls Cheer Squad had huddled together after spotting Iris's pom-pom rainbow moments ago. Now they broke apart to do a thank-you cheer for her that they'd made up on the spur of the moment.

"Go, Iris, go!

We love your rainbow!

Your colors inspire us.

You rock, Goddess Iris!"

Iris grinned and waved back. Antheia laughed and waved too.

"Make me a trident rainbow for good luck!" a boy called out to Iris. It was Poseidon, the godboy of the sea. He was holding up his trident, which was a fancy three-pronged pitchfork that dripped seawater. He and a godboy named Ares were downfield, having a contest to see who could throw the farthest. As Iris watched, Ares chucked his spear halfway down the field, and a roar went up from the boys who'd gathered around to cheer both him and Poseidon on.

Quickly Iris tossed out some magic and created a

trident-shaped rainbow for Poseidon, then a spear rainbow for Ares. More requests came, and she continued making rainbows to represent the sports that different godboys and goddessgirls were doing on the fields. With each new design the other students erupted into whoops and clapping.

When she shaped a bow and arrow rainbow in the sky, a boy shouted, "Nice!" It was the dark-haired, dark-eyed godboy Apollo. He usually practiced archery with his twin sister, Artemis. But since she was doing Cheer, he was practicing with Eros, who was also amazing with a bow and arrow.

The golden-winged Eros was concentrating on a distant target now, the string of his bow drawn back. When he released his arrow, it flew straight to the target's heart. *Zing!* Iris and Antheia watched Apollo punch a fist into the air in approval. Afterward he said something to Eros, then turned and jogged toward the two girls, clutching a rolled-up piece of papyrus in one fist.

Iris sensed Antheia's excitement rise and saw her cheeks redden. As would be obvious to anyone, Antheia was blushing. However, only Iris could also see the air around her friend turning a pale rosy-red color. This was an aura, which was sort of a full-body halo. All her life Iris had been able to see colorful auras like this around people, which indicated their emotions or moods. After years of practice, she knew what the different shades of an aura meant. For instance, a deep red one meant embarrassment.

However the air around Antheia was turning the kind of pale rosy-red that indicated liking. *Uh-oh.* Though Iris wasn't as good as Aphrodite at divining who was in like with who, she knew what this particular aura meant. It meant that Antheia hadn't given up on her dream of Apollo becoming her crush. Unfortunately.

"I was wondering if you'd add some decoration to this letterscroll for me," Apollo asked Iris when he reached the two girls. "Artemis said you're good at doing fancy decorations. And I wanted this letter to be more colorful, you know?"

Iris wasn't surprised by this request. MOA students often asked her to add colorful flourishes to the borders of special letters, or even to do face-painting at times. She might not have been a fine artist, but her talent with colors extended to special decorative touches. She'd added embellishments to lockers, dorm room walls and bulletin boards, and even to secret notescrolls students passed in class or left in someone's locker.

She darted a glance at Antheia. Iris was sure that the scroll Apollo held out to her was meant for a mortal princess named Cassandra. Had Antheia guessed this too?

Cassandra's family owned the bakery that made Oracle-O fortune cookies in the Immortal Marketplace, which was located below Mount Olympus and had shops that sold everything from the newest Greek fashions to yarn, cosmetics, and thunderbolts. Cassandra's family lived in an apartment above their shop.

"Hi, Apollo," Antheia suddenly piped up in a hopeful voice that was higher than her usual one.

Iris groaned silently. That girl just would not give up! She couldn't seem to accept that her dreams of Apollo ever like-liking her were doomed. Everyone knew he was in like with Cassandra. But that fact hadn't stopped Antheia from wishing it could be otherwise.

"Oh, hi, Antheia," Apollo replied, looking a little uncomfortable. His aura had turned yellow-green, which suggested to Iris that he suspected Antheia's crush but was too cowardly to tell her that he wasn't interested in returning her affection. Godboys were mostly strong and forthright when it came to sports or battle, but crushes were a subject they usually tried to avoid.

"How about asking Aphrodite to add something cute, instead?" Iris suggested to him. "Maybe some hearts and stuff. She's the goddess of love after all." If she didn't take the scroll he held out, maybe he'd leave quickly so her friend could calm down. Poor Antheia. Iris had tried hinting to her that her fixation on Apollo was impossible, but Antheia just didn't seem to get it. So Iris simply did what she could to discourage her friend's doomed crush. She even pointed out other cute and interesting guys now and then with the hope of steering her toward another boy.

"Well, she's busy with Cheer, and I'm kind of in

a hurry to send this letterscroll to . . . someone," said Apollo.

Beside her, Antheia looked momentarily elated.

Ye gods! thought Iris. Was she actually hoping he meant the scroll for her? This was not good!

"Hermes should be here any minute," Apollo said. Looking up, his brown eyes scanned the skies for the delivery chariot that flew to MOA at least once every day carrying packages and letters. "I'm hoping to send my letterscroll to the IM with him." After a slight hesitation and an awkward glance at Antheia, he added, "It's for Cassandra."

Instantly Antheia wilted, looking like Apollo had just shot down her hopes with one of his arrows. So she really had been daydreaming that he'd planned to give her the letterscroll. Surely she must know better. Still, Iris knew what it was like to hope for something so hard. And with all her heart she wanted to believe that her dream of becoming the goddess of rainbows wasn't as doomed as Antheia's crush on Apollo.

Sensing that the insistent godboy wasn't going to give up, Iris gave in and said, "Okay, sure, I'll decorate it for you." She took his scroll over to the bleachers near where the Cheer Squad was practicing, while Antheia and Apollo followed. She always carried a set of preloaded colored-ink pens around just in case, and now she whipped them from the bag she'd left on the bleachers. She chose three pens—a bright blue, a flamingo-pink, and a lime-green.

Quickly she unrolled and flattened the scroll face-down on a bench seat so no one could accidentally read the private message on its other side. Then she proceeded to draw a cute border on the outside of the letterscroll with the three different-colored pens at once, adding rainbows, bows and arrows, and swirly flourishes.

After a few minutes she glanced over at Apollo, who had been admiring her work. "Want me to draw her name on the outside too?" Although she was in a hurry for him to go, she wanted to do a good job.

Apollo nodded enthusiastically. "That would be mega-cool!" While he watched Iris form and decorate the letters of Cassandra's name, Antheia stared at him with a besotted expression.

Seeming to sense her gaze, he looked over at her. "Nice day, huh?"

Antheia blushed. "Um, yeah. For a Sunday."

Which didn't really make much sense, thought Iris. Antheia seemed too head over heels in like right now to notice that, though. And she didn't have a chance to say more to him because just then an MOA goddessgirl named Pheme zipped over. She'd arrived almost out of nowhere, it seemed, her sandaled feet hovering a few inches above the ground.

As she touched down, the small, glittery wings on her back stilled. Iris had always had wings, but Pheme's wings were a recent gift from Principal Zeus, which made them extra special—a reward for heroism during a fiery battle. The girl's wings were a cute shade of orange, the same as her lip gloss and short, spiky hair. Iris's wings were cute too, but unlike Pheme's, they were too delicate for flying. Like her rainbows, they were decorative, not functional.

"What's wrong with you?" Pheme asked Antheia first thing upon landing.

Oh no, thought Iris. She must've noticed how Antheia was mooning over Apollo. Pheme was the goddess of gossip and rumor, so you had to be careful around her. She noticed everything, and telling her anything was the same as shouting it to the whole school!

"Nothing's wrong with her," Iris answered for her suddenly tongue-tied best friend.

"Come on. She's blushing. What's up?" Pheme was studying Antheia in a super-interested snoopy way now. As always, when the gossipy girl spoke, puffy cloud-letters formed above her head so that anyone who happened to be looking could read her words.

Seeking out juicy gossip and sniffing out rumors was sort of like Pheme's job at the Academy. Plus, it gave her material for the gossip column she wrote in *Teen Scrollazine*, which was a mega-popular 'zine read by mortals and immortals alike.

Iris finished her drawing and stood, handing the letterscroll to Apollo. "This is perfect!" he proclaimed, smiling down at her work.

"What's perfect?" The Cheer Squad had taken a break, and Artemis had come over to talk to Apollo. She peered at the name on the letterscroll, then rolled her eyes at her brother in a teasing way. "For your crush, I see."

"What of it?" said Apollo, blushing.

"I want to read it!" Artemis made a playful grab for the scroll, but he held it away, high above his head so she couldn't nab it.

He smiled at Iris in thanks, and then flashed a quick grin of farewell at Antheia. "See you!"

Antheia sighed softly, watching him go. Iris touched her friend's arm, lending support. Truth was, Iris had once like-liked Apollo too. At first he'd seemed the perfect fit for her. He was into poetry and she was good with rhyme and colorful writing. He was interested in weather, especially the sun; and you needed sunlight to make a rainbow. For a while Iris had thought they were destined for each other.

But then, Antheia had suddenly announced to Iris

that *she* liked Apollo. It hadn't been easy, but Iris had backed off without even telling Antheia about her crush on him.

She looked over at Pheme, who had begun quizzing Artemis about the squad's new cheers. It was really lucky that she hadn't guessed about Iris's and Antheia's crushes on Apollo. Lucky also that she hadn't guessed when Iris had gotten her very first crush back in sixth grade. On Poseidon.

Many of the girls at MOA had liked the turquoise godboy of the sea at one time or another. That is, until they'd figured out he was as shallow as the pools in the fanciful water fountains he designed around the Academy and on Earth. So it wasn't really all that surprising when Antheia had declared in sixth grade that she liked Poseidon—*before* Iris could say it first. Iris had backed off then, too.

They were best buds, and as far as Iris was concerned, that meant you didn't steal each other's crushes. However, she really wished they'd stop liking the same guys!

As far as her more recent crush on Apollo went, it had turned out that he was more into sports and the telling of prophecies and fortunes than into weather science and magic and color, as Iris was. They didn't have much in common after all. Cassandra, on the other hand, was way into fortune-telling. So she and Apollo really were perfect for each other. And unfortunately for Antheia, during a recent event involving a magic carousel at the Immortal Marketplace, Apollo had decided he liked Cassandra.

"Hey!" Apollo yelled when he was halfway back to the target-shooting range. Iris turned to look and saw that a sudden gust of wind had whooshed the letterscroll right out of his hands. It flew a dozen feet up in the air, where it was tossed and tumbled end over end, before being shot across the sky and flung high into the bleachers. "Hey!" he yelled again. He was chasing it now, coming back toward her, Antheia, and the other girls. He took the steps up the bleachers two at a time, but just as he got close enough to grab his scroll, another gust snatched it away.

"Wow! The wind's picking up," Pheme noted. All around the sports fields, trees were swaying, and leaves on the ground were whirling in small tornados.

"Godsamighty! You're not kidding," said Artemis when a sudden gust knocked her into Antheia.

"I wonder what's causing it," mused Iris. She pushed back strands of her hair that had blown into her face, and looked at the sky, half-expecting to see Hermes in his delivery service chariot dipping lower. Sure enough, she spotted his chariot. But it was leaving

MOA, a speck disappearing into the distance, and was too far away to have created such a strong breeze.

"Drat," said Apollo. He'd paused in his chase to look up as well. He was obviously disappointed to see that he'd missed Hermes' daily pickup and delivery already.

"Whoa!" squealed Aphrodite. Iris looked over to the far end of the bleachers to see that an unusually strong gust had tangled the girl's long golden hair. Now another rush of wind whisked Apollo's letter-scroll toward Iris's group. When it landed by their feet, Artemis picked it up.

Apollo loped down the bleachers, taking them two at a time again, till he stood before Artemis. "I missed Hermes. And Zeus asked me to catalog some poetry in the library today, so I can't take the scroll to the IM myself," he said. He held out a hand toward her, motioning for her to give him the scroll.

Shooting him a mischievous grin, Artemis held it away. "What about our archery practice?" she asked with a raised eyebrow.

"Sorry, Sis. Okay if we skip it? I already promised Zeus to do that library stuff." He made a grab for the scroll, but she was too fast and held on. But then, seeming to take pity on him, she nodded and handed it over.

Apollo tapped one end of the scroll in his opposite palm. "I really wanted to get this to Cassandra this morning. It's—" Noticing that Pheme was there, he clammed up.

"Why not call up a magic wind to take it to her?" suggested Artemis. Magic winds were random breezes or small gusts of wind that came when summoned and delivered letterscrolls here and there. However, truly important documents and messages, and heavy packages, were usually entrusted to Hermes.

Before Apollo could reply, Antheia blurted, "Iris and I are going to the IM. We can take your letterscroll for you."

Apollo brightened. "Really? That'd be great. Thanks!" He handed the scroll to Iris, who stood closest to him.

Startled, Iris took it, glancing at Antheia in surprise as Apollo took off for the library. The girls had made no plans to visit the IM. After a morning on the sports fields, they'd talked about getting lunch in the MOA cafeteria, then hanging out in the dorm room they shared on the fourth floor of the Academy. So why had Antheia said that?

Iris could sense that Pheme's nosy-o-meter was on high alert. So far the spiky-haired girl hadn't seemed to guess what was up with Antheia's one-sided crush. And feeling protective of her BFF, Iris did not want Pheme to figure it out.

Iris was good at keeping secrets, so she'd never understood Pheme's complete inability to safeguard them for even two seconds. But the gossipy girl couldn't help it she supposed. Any more than the other girls could help their talents, like Persephone's ability to make things grow or Athena's gift for figuring out difficult math problems.

Hoping to distract Pheme, Iris shoved Apollo's scroll into her bag and then drew her arm back. She sent a new ball of magic hurtling high into the air. *Brrrng!* In mere seconds a traditional arched rainbow arced across the sky. It stretched so far that it was impossible to see where it ended!

Gasps sounded across the fields. And whoops of surprise and delight. It was the first time Iris had managed such a huge rainbow, so she was kind of delighted herself.

"Wow! I think that one almost made it to Earth," said Pheme, excitedly taking notes for her gossip column.

"Yeah, cool," Artemis agreed.

Antheia leaned close and whispered encouragingly to Iris, "With Pheme around to spread the word, Principal You-Know-Who is bound to hear about it and be impressed."

Iris nodded, feeling excited about her chances. "And when the moment is right, I'll spring the big question on him!" She changed her voice slightly, pretending she was asking him right then: "How about making me Goddess of Rainbows, Principal Zeus?"

She and Antheia giggled.

"What did you just say about 'sensible juice'?" Pheme interrupted, having misunderstood Iris's last two words.

With a wink at Iris, Antheia corrected Pheme. "No, she said, 'bendable spruce.'" She pointed at the trees that were still whooshing in the wind. Then she went on chatting with Pheme, trying to throw her off the gossip track.

But Iris barely heard. She reached out to touch the fantastic rainbow she'd made. Was this one solid enough? she wondered. Did she dare try . . . riding it?

"WHO DID THAT!" boomed a thunderous voice.

Iris jumped in surprise. So did everyone else on the fields. Then, like all the other students, she looked up to see the one, the only—Principal Zeus! He was flying high overhead, his wild red hair blowing in the wind as he rode his white-winged thunderbolt-carrying horse, Pegasus, across the sky. Returning from duties down on Earth no doubt. Zeus was a busy and powerful guy. Not only was he the principal of the Academy. He was also King of the Gods and Ruler of the Heavens!

"I said, WHO DID THAT!" Zeus repeated, sounding even crankier now. He was pointing at her rainbow. Everyone turned to stare at Iris. A hush settled over the sports fields.

Oops! Iris's eyes widened as she realized what she'd almost done. Or rather, what her huge rainbow had almost done. On its way through the clouds, apparently, it had nearly beaned Zeus!

His bushy red eyebrows bunched into a V-shape and he frowned more deeply now. At her! The muscles in his arms bulged as he held the reins of mighty Pegasus, and sunlight flashed off the wide gold bands he wore around his wrists. Sparks of electricity prickled around him, a sure sign he was angry.

"You dare try to strike me with your rainbow!" Zeus roared at her.

"Strike you? No . . . Uh, I," mumbled Iris, too scared to form a sensible reply loud enough for him to hear.

"My office! Twenty minutes!" he commanded.

Gulp! So much for this being a happy day! thought Iris.

2
The Four Winds

As ZEUS RODE ON TOWARD THE ACADEMY'S main building, Antheia and Iris stared at each other with big, worried eyes. "Want me to go with you?" Antheia offered generously.

Iris took a deep breath, still feeling rather stunned. She'd never, ever, ever been called to the principal's office for doing something wrong before. "That's okay," she said. "I don't want to get you in trouble too."

"Don't worry. His boom is worse than his bite," Athena assured Iris. She'd come over to Artemis and was tossing her pom-poms down onto the bottom bleacher.

"Thanks," said Iris, taking heart. "I guess you ought to know, since he's your dad."

Athena, who'd begun attending MOA only that year, grinned. "Mm-hm, but I can imagine how you feel," she admitted. "Even I was scared to death the first time I walked into his office."

"We've all been there and come out alive, though," Persephone reassured Iris. She and Aphrodite had drifted over as well, pom-poms in hand. All four goddessgirls on the Cheer Squad wore matching GG charm necklaces that gleamed and sparkled in the sunlight.

"Eek!" Aphrodite let out a shriek as the wind began

to whoosh again. Her beautiful, long hair lifted out behind her in a golden fan. There were more shrieks across the fields as the sudden strong breeze whipped up chitons and tunics, and students struggled to tug them down.

"Look! Up in the heavens!" someone shouted.

Everyone looked up to see four winged godboys overhead, each riding on the separate forceful wind he controlled as they headed toward the sports fields.

"The four winds? No wonder it's so crazy windy out here all of a sudden!" said Antheia.

Iris swung around to gaze at her rainbows, worried at what she'd see. Sure enough, all the designs she'd made were now wobbling in the sky. Rainbows should *not* wobble. That was one of the things she was trying to learn to control. Until she could make her rainbows stronger and sturdier, she'd never dare try to ride them.

Traveling via rainbow would surely be a useful thing and prove her talent. But if a rainbow wobbled in the middle of a ride, she'd come crashing down.

The four godboys and their swirling winds were rapidly moving closer. Although they were as high as the clouds, the effects of their approach were growing ever stronger down below. Eros's target fell over, and Apollo ran to help him right it. The gusts had grown so forceful by now that some students were sent tumbling head over heels. And these were *not* students who'd been practicing gymnastics!

"Back off, blowhards!" yelled Poseidon, shaking his trident at the windy godboys.

By now they had practically destroyed Iris's big, amazing rainbow. And all of her other cleverly shaped rainbows too.

Suddenly one of the wind-boys winged lower, sending

a chill over the entire field. Iris shivered. She, Antheia, Pheme, and the four Cheer Squad goddessgirls huddled together near the bleachers for warmth. This had to be Boreas. In Science-ology class they'd all learned that he controlled the cold wind of winter. Now the white-haired boy's frosty breath blew away the last bit of color from Iris's fading rainbows. On purpose!

"I huffed and puffed and blew your rainbows away," he called out to her. Then he laughed.

Hmph! She felt like huffing herself. And she never huffed. "Poseidon is right. Those boys really *are* blow-hards!" she grumbled to herself. Boreas had turned the air so freezing cold that she could see her own breath as she spoke.

Just then one of the windy godboys—this one had brown hair—called to Boreas. With a final whoosh of frigid breath, the white-haired godboy rose and rejoined his brothers. Iris had learned about them in Science-ology too. Zephyr controlled the warm west wind of spring, Notus ruled the hot south wind of summer, and Eurus was in charge of the cool east wind of autumn.

"Ye gods! Why are *they* here?" Persephone wondered aloud, holding her hair and the hem of her chiton so they didn't whip up. Most of the others girls were doing the same.

"Yeah, I thought it was against the rules for those godboys to travel together," Iris said, raising her voice. By now everyone was practically yelling to be heard over the strong, loud swirl of the tumultuous winds.

Aphrodite nodded. "Me too. Because having them all here, blowing winds of different temperatures, could cause a weather incident."

Iris and Antheia shared a grin. Aphrodite called even the most important events "incidents." When the beautiful goddessgirl had caused Paris and Helen to fall in love, thereby accidentally causing the Trojan War, she'd called that an incident too.

"Something's up," Pheme said. "And I'm going to find out what it is," Her nosy-o-meter was obviously spinning as wildly as those winds! Flapping her wings hard so as not to be blown away, she followed the winds toward the Academy.

Others began leaving the fields to do the same, including Iris and Antheia. "Pheme's right," said Antheia. "Something is *definitely* up."

"Mm-hm," Iris agreed as they and the Cheer Squad hurried toward the Academy. She had a feeling things were about to turn stormy at MOA.

However, she was almost glad of the distraction. Because it was taking her mind off her upcoming meeting with Zeus. As she and everyone else dashed for the school courtyard to see what was going on, there were more shrieks from the group as the winds continued to make trouble. Along the way, gusts lifted Iris off her feet now and then.

"I don't suppose they could be bringing Lonely Hearts letterscrolls to you," Persephone called to Aphrodite. The wind snatched her words and blew them back to Iris's ears.

"All four of them? Just to bring me a few letters? I don't think so," Aphrodite replied. She regularly received letters about crush troubles from both mortals and immortals who joined her Lonely Hearts Club.

"For sure," Athena agreed. "Those boys have bigger things to do with their winds. Like whooshing them around to change the seasons."

It was true, Iris knew. The winds were busy around the world throughout winter, spring, summer, and fall, which was the reason they always sent the smaller magic breezes to carry mail and simple messages to and from immortals.

Iris and the others soon reached the marble-tiled courtyard in front of the majestic Mount Olympus Academy. Built of polished white stone and standing atop the highest mountain in Greece, the Academy was five stories tall and surrounded on all sides by dozens of Ionic columns. Low-relief friezes had been sculpted just below the building's peaked rooftop. Normally the MOA gleamed in the sunlight. But the skies were gloomy now, lending its marble walls a gray cast.

Iris, Antheia, Pheme, and the four Cheer Squad goddessgirls came to a halt in the courtyard and stared in amazement at everything being tossed topsy-turvy. Scrolls were ripped from students' hands. Hair whipped and tangled. Potted plants and statues crashed over onto their sides. It was all the girls could do to keep from getting blown over themselves as the four windy god-boys touched down!

Some of the teachers had come outside the Academy to check things out, including Hera, who was Zeus's wife and Athena's stepmom. Occasionally she taught a class at MOA, but mainly she kept busy running Hera's Happy Endings, a wedding store in the Immortal Marketplace.

Boreas, Zephyr, Notus, and Eurus, whooshed up the Academy's granite steps. The big bronze front doors opened, and Mr. Cyclops, the one-eyed Hero-ology teacher, stepped out. He greeted the four windy boys in a harsh, reprimanding tone. He was obviously as annoyed as Iris and her friends about the havoc they were wreaking.

However, after listening to whatever the windy brothers had to say, his expression changed. Now he looked grim and sort of stunned too. He held the enormous front doors wide and stepped aside. "Hurry!" he told them, quickly waving them past. He also said something else that Iris couldn't hear, then finished with, "He'll want to hear your news."

The four windy gods whooshed past the teacher and inside MOA. Once the door slammed shut behind them, all was calm again. Immediately Aphrodite whipped out a white alabaster comb and began running it through her tangled golden hair.

As Mr. Cyclops continued to stand at the top of the stairs, the single big eyeball in the middle of his forehead scanned the crowd of students assembled in the courtyard below. "Excitement's over! Go back to whatever you were doing," he instructed. Then, along with the other teachers, he turned and went inside.

"Did anybody hear what the winds told Mr. Cyclops?" Pheme asked everyone, darting among the crowd in the courtyard. But no one had. For a moment her wings drooped with disappointment, but then they sprang back up. She'd probably remembered she could still spread the word about Iris's nearly bonking Zeus with a rainbow!

Iris glanced at the courtyard sundial. Her twenty minutes were nearly up. "I guess I'd better go inside too," she said to Antheia and the other four goddess-girls. "And head for Zeus's—*Zzzt!*–office—*Zzzt!*" With each *Zzzt!* sound she made, she pressed her index finger to her opposite arm and gave a shocked little jump, pretending Zeus was zapping her with electricity for her wrongdoing out on the fields.

"I'm sure it'll be okay," Athena assured her again as she and her friends moved back out toward the sports fields.

"Good luck," Aphrodite called in her bright beautiful voice. By now she'd almost tamed her hair.

Persephone sent Iris a smile of encouragement, and Artemis gave her a thumbs-up. Even though they were mega-popular, these four goddessgirls weren't at all stuck-up.

"What about Apollo's letterscroll? Want me to deliver it to the IM for you?" asked Antheia.

Iris glanced down at the bag she still clutched in one hand. In all the excitement, she'd momentarily forgotten about the scroll. "Since Apollo entrusted his message to me, I'd better do it. If I'm still alive after seeing Principal Zeus, we can go to the IM together." She gave a nervous little laugh, though she didn't think the part about Zeus was funny one bit.

"Did I just hear you say you're going to the IM?" asked a woman's voice.

Both girls turned to see Hera standing there. Apparently, she hadn't gone back inside with the other teachers. As usual, her thick blond hair was styled high upon her head. Iris had always thought she was a good match for Zeus, with her regal bearing. Although she wasn't unusually tall, something about her made her seem statuesque. Probably her confidence.

When both girls nodded, Hera stepped closer. She was holding a scroll, Iris noticed. "Then would you deliver this letterscroll to the IM for me? I'm too busy to go myself. Zeus and I are visiting, um . . . That is, we have an appointment that will take us away from Mount Olympus today. And it's important that this message gets delivered this morning." She sounded anxious.

"Okay," said Iris.

"Thank you. And please, don't tell Zeu– um, anyone about this," Hera added in a quiet voice. Then she stuck the scroll into Iris's free hand, rushed up the granite steps, and pushed in through MOA's bronze front doors to enter the Academy.

Iris and Antheia looked at each other in surprise. "Did she almost say 'don't tell Zeus'?" Iris asked.

"That's what I thought too," said Antheia. "I wonder what's in that letterscroll that she doesn't want him to know? And why didn't she give the scroll to Hermes earlier when he was here?"

"She must've accidentally missed him like Apollo did," Iris said. This whole message delivery system wasn't working, she decided right then and there. Having Hermes come to MOA only once a day (except for the occasional special delivery) obviously wasn't often enough. Not with all these urgent messages to be sent. If she had the nerve, she'd speak to the principal about it. Ha! Not likely.

"Or maybe Hera didn't *want* to give it to Hermes

because he's loyal to Zeus. And Zeus might worm secret information out of him," said Antheia.

Both girls peered at Hera's scroll curiously, and Iris read the writing on the outside of it aloud. "'To Ceyx, Immortal Marketplace.'"

"Never heard of him," said Antheia.

"Me either. How am I supposed to find him with only a name to go on?"

Just then they heard Zeus's loud voice boom from an open window on the main floor—his office window. "What!" he yelled. Both girls jumped a little, even though he wasn't yelling at them.

"Somebody's in a bad mood," said Antheia.

Iris cringed. "Think that's about me? Could he really be that mad about my rainbow almost beaning him?"

"I hope not," said Antheia.

"Yeah, maybe he's just yelling at those windy godboys

for causing all this mess," said Iris, glancing around at the chaos in the courtyard.

Antheia nodded. But she looked as uncertain about that as Iris felt.

Iris stuffed Hera's scroll into her bag with Apollo's and headed up the front steps. Minutes later she stood in the hall staring at a door with the words "FRONT OFFICE" chiseled on it. She went inside.

Ms. Hydra, Zeus's nine-headed administrative assistant, was standing behind her tall desk. Beyond her was another door. The one that led to Zeus's office. The assistant was busy helping a group of students that had gathered around her. Everyone looked a little jittery. And no wonder! Even though Zeus's office door was shut, every few seconds Iris could hear loud banging and thumping noises beyond it.

"What's going on in there!" Iris murmured under her breath.

"Just the four winds," Ms. Hydra's pink head replied without looking away from the papers she was working on. The head obviously had good hearing. Which made sense. That head's nickname was Pinky, and it was almost as gossipy as Pheme.

So Iris had been right in guessing that this was where those windbag boys had come after they'd entered the school. Here to Zeus's office! Mr. Cyclops must've been saying it was Zeus who'd want to hear the four winds' news, whatever it was.

"I'm supposed to see the principal too," she told Ms. Hydra's gray head. It was her worrywart head, and the only one that wasn't currently busy. At the sound of a sudden loud thump, the head swung around on its long neck to gaze at Zeus's door. "Maybe you should come back another time," it advised Iris.

For half a second Iris considered bailing. But then

she shook her head. "I wish I could. But he told me to come, so I'd better stay."

"Well, then, please sign in," said the gray head, which was also the most efficient of the heads. "We're trying to get Zeus organized, so I'm keeping track of who visits his office and how he spends his time." It nodded toward a sign-in book that Iris hadn't noticed on the desktop.

Immediately Iris whipped out her set of pens and began to sign her name in a fancy way, using a different-color pen for each decorative letter.

"Oh dear," said the gray worrywart head, watching Iris write. "I'm a little concerned that such elaborate writing won't fit on the line and will take up too much space on the page."

Ms. Hydra's smiley yellow head leaned over to admire Iris's work. "I think it's colorful and absolutely lovely."

Iris managed a shaky smile in return, but it

disappeared from her face when Zeus's door suddenly blew open. She whirled around and pressed back against the tall desk as the wind began whisking things off it and sending them flying around the lobby.

"Everyone out!" all of Ms. Hydra's heads chorused at once to the students she'd been helping. Her heads bobbing and weaving, she slithered out from behind her desk and began chasing down the papers.

Since Iris dared not leave without seeing Zeus, she stayed to help too, chasing some papers all the way to his door.

"So Typhon has escaped Tartarus," she overheard Zeus saying. "I locked that beast up after the war with the Titans for a very good reason. He presents a terrible threat if he's coming this way."

Typhon? Who's he? Iris wondered, straightening and clutching an armful of papers to her chest. They'd never studied such a creature in Beast-ology class. Trying to act casual so as not to draw attention to herself, she moved nearer to Zeus's open door to listen.

"He's a monster all right," one of the windy boys was saying.

"A tornado with winds of epic proportions, greater than all four of us put together," said a second wind.

"He's been on a rampage, destroying villages," added a third wind. "But now he's gone into hiding. It's like he's waiting for something."

"I wish we knew what he was up to," said the fourth wind.

"Following the orders of whoever released him from Tartarus, no doubt. And I'm going to find out who that was, if it's the last thing I do!" Zeus proclaimed. *Boom! Zzzt! Zzzt!* Iris's breath caught in alarm at the sound. The faint smell of smoke drifted to her nose. Zeus must've slammed his fist on his desk to emphasize his point and zapped the surrounding area. She hoped that didn't happen when her turn came to face him!

"Typhon's not the brightest beast I've ever locked up in Tartarus," Zeus went on. "That works in our favor but also makes him unpredictable. It's impossible to know how or when he might strike. And what he lacks in brains he makes up for in brute strength."

Tartarus was the most awful place in the Underworld, where truly evil people and creatures wound up. As far as Iris knew, no one—except this Typhon monster—had ever escaped that awful pit of despair.

"The safety of everyone on Mount Olympus is at stake!" Zeus said at last.

The conversation she'd overheard rattled Iris. The four winds seemed to have come to MOA to report that a monstrous fiend called Typhon was on the way. But apparently they didn't know when he'd appear or how to stop him. The truly scary part was that Zeus didn't seem to know either. Everyone on Mount Olympus and Earth counted on him to take care of such things and to save them from disaster. She shuddered. Was it possible that this was one disaster he couldn't fix?

As the four winds began arguing about how to fight Typhon, objects started to whirl around the lobby again. Gusts snatched away some of the papers Iris had collected and knocked the sign-in book from Ms. Hydra's desktop onto the floor. By now the assistant's nine heads were bobbling every which way, trying to figure out which mess to clean up first.

"CALM DOWN!" Zeus boomed at the boys. The windy brothers gasped in awe of his mighty authority, and the strength of their indrawn breaths pulled the door shut. *Slam!* And then Iris could hear no more.

Just as she and Ms. Hydra finally finished setting the outer office to rights, the door to Zeus's office opened again and the four winds trooped out past Iris. She decided that the boys must be able to control the strength of their winds, because now they hardly blew at all.

Ms. Hydra pushed the sign-in book across her desktop toward one of the boys as he passed. "Zephyr? Your brothers signed in, but I need your signature as well."

"Sure," Zephyr said in a friendly tone. He flicked his head up and to the side in a quick movement that pushed his wavy chestnut-brown hair off his forehead. Iris couldn't help noticing how cute his blue wings and clear sky-blue eyes were. He looked around, then glanced at Ms. Hydra. "Got a pen?"

"I do," Iris announced, opening her bag and volunteering her set.

Zephyr grinned at her, choosing a lime-green pen. "Thanks." As he wrote his name, he must've taken note of her fancy writing on the line above in the sign-in book. Because when he handed her pen back, he asked, "You Iris?"

She nodded. "Um-hm. Hi! Welcome to MOA!" *Argh!* Why had she blurted *that* out? It wasn't as if he and his brothers were *enrolling* here. Still, it was only polite to welcome newcomers to the Academy, right? Even if they wouldn't be staying permanently.

"Figured," said Zephyr. "Because of your pens and all." He gave her a warm smile, and this time she smiled back.

Boreas leaned over to study the colorful pen set she still held. "What, no frosty white or silver gray in there, Susie Sunshine? Those are my favorite ink colors. So much more dignified. I know what I'm talking about. I won the penmanship award three years in a row at our school."

Iris shivered and stepped back. Not only was he a cold wind, but he was boastful, too! Her choice of pen colors reflected her happy personality. She knew she could be pretty cheery all the time and that it annoyed some people. Well, too bad! Because that was who she was. And it was certainly better than being gloomy all the time, or being annoying like him.

She cocked her head and joked to all four winds, "Not Susie Sunshine. More like Rachel Rainbows."

"Or more like Harpy . . . um," Boreas began, but then he paused, seemingly stumped for an *H* nickname to add after "Harpy."

Did that mean these brothers knew that her three sisters were Harpies, even though she didn't look at all like them? she wondered. Even some of the students at MOA didn't know that! Although her sisters had pretty faces and normal hair, their bodies were feathered, and they had bird-claw feet, and could fly. Together they owned the Hungry, Hungry Harpy Café in the IM. And they were supercranky—pretty much the opposite of her personality.

Not willing to let Boreas know he'd embarrassed her by mentioning them, she smiled brightly. "The Happy Harpy?" His brothers and even Ms. Hydra's yellow head laughed at that. "But I'm not—"

"Never mind," Boreas muttered before she could say she wasn't actually a Harpy. He seemed irritated that she'd gotten the last word. "C'mon, guys."

"See you," Iris said politely. *Ha-ha!* Boreas might be the cold wind, but by keeping a cool head, she'd bested him. Zephyr caught her eye and sent her another warm smile. As he turned to leave the office, he lifted a hand behind his back, giving her a thumbs-up.

"Hey, keep up, Zephyr!" Boreas called back to him, and Iris watched the brown-haired boy scurry to rejoin his brothers.

"Come along, Iris!" urged Ms. Hydra.

Iris looked over to see that the assistant's impatient purple head was speaking to her. "Don't want to keep the principal waiting. *Hup! Hup!* Get moving!"

As Iris passed into Zeus's office, the impatient head called after her, "Be quick about your business. Principal Zeus is a busy guy. And he has an appointment with Hera in fifteen minutes."

"Okay." Iris reluctantly trudged into Zeus's domain. How would he punish her for almost striking him and Pegasus with her misguided rainbow? she wondered. Blast her to smithereens with one of his thunderbolts? Zap her silly with the electric sparks that shot from his fingertips?

And that wasn't the only thing worrying her. Hera's scroll was burning a hole in her pocket—er, bag. What if Zeus guessed she had it? He was powerful. Would he see right through her and know there was something she wasn't telling him? She wished Hera hadn't put her in this position! But her message must be something super-important, and Iris wouldn't let her down.

Unlike Pheme, she took secrets seriously, but keeping one from the King of the Gods was making her *seriously* uncomfortable. She wished she didn't have to!

3

A Mission

AT FIRST IRIS DIDN'T SEE ZEUS BECAUSE OF THE jungle of stuff that filled his office and the towering file cabinets that sat in the middle of it like buildings in a clutter city. Rumor had it that his office was messy. But this was worse than she'd imagined. Had the winds caused this, or did his office always look like a tornado had hit it?

While searching for the principal, she spied stacks of scrolls here and there and stepped over discarded oddball art projects, including what appeared to be a partly mashed architect's model of Zeus's great temple in the city of Olympia on Earth. She'd never been there to see it herself, but she knew that the gigantic ivory-and-gold statue of him inside the temple was one of the Seven Wonders of the world.

She stepped over a map of Greece and two board games, and then crunched three half-empty bottles of Zeus Juice underfoot. One file cabinet had been overturned, its side dented in as though it had suffered a mighty blow from a meaty fist. *Gulp!*

"Ibis?" the principal boomed, making her jump.

Huh? Had Zeus just called her "Ibis"? No, she must've misheard. Although, come to think of it, he was notoriously bad at names. So he'd either gotten her name wrong or he really did think that she looked like a long-legged, long-beaked wading bird!

"Coming," she called in a jittery voice that sounded scared even to her. She rounded another cabinet to discover Zeus sitting on a huge golden throne behind an even bigger desk. He held a four-foot tall, solid gold Best God-Dad in the Universe trophy sideways in one hand and was lifting it up and down as he studied a scrollmap that lay open on his desk. The trophy must be something Athena had given him. How sweet! His muscled arm flexed, and electricity fizzled from his fingertips, making the trophy sizzle and pop. He looked like something was on his mind. Mayhem? Involving her?

Suddenly he glanced up, pinning her with his electric-blue eyes. "Sit," he commanded, gesturing to the six chairs facing his desk. He dropped the trophy to the floor. *Thunk!*

Iris sat in the nearest chair. *Crunch!* She half-stood again and saw she'd just smashed a bag of ambrosia chips that had been lying on the seat cushion.

"Oh, sorry," she mumbled. She moved over to the next chair. This one's cushion had two holes with scorch marks around them. Come to think of it, there were scorch marks on all six chairs as well as on most of the walls and other stuff, she realized. From Zeus hurling thunderbolts at his visitors? A shiver ran down her spine as she sat again. She set her bag on her lap, then tucked her fingers under the sides of her legs to hide their trembling.

As she awaited her doom, she upside-down-read the title of the map on Zeus's desk and discovered it was a map of the route to the infamous Gray Ladies' office. Why was he studying that? The Gray Ladies were the school counselors. No one who went to their office in a faraway land ever talked afterward about what had happened there, so she'd always figured it must be an awful place no one wanted to think about. *Godsamighty!* He wasn't sending her there, was he?

Principal Zeus shoved the scrollmap to one side and folded his beefy hands on top of his desk. "I've been keeping an eye on you, Ibis," he announced.

"Iris," she corrected, then wished she hadn't. Who cared what he called her? Maybe if he decided to banish her from MOA, he'd tell Ms. Hydra to banish Ibis, and then no one would put two and two together and figure out he actually meant *her*.

Wait! She had to calm down. Had to convince him to forget what had happened with her rainbow out on the field. Not only that, but this might be her only chance to talk him into naming her the Goddess of Rainbows. Because how often did an opportunity to chat with the King of the Gods and Ruler of the Heavens one on one come along? Not very.

"About that rainbow incident," she began in a rush.

"About those rainbows of yours," he said at almost the same time.

"I know, I know. I didn't mean to almost hit you with that big rainbow I made. I'm really sorry," she went on before he could beat her to the punch. "But practice makes perfect, right?"

"Practicing something you're interested in improving—like a rainbow—is a worthy goal, but maybe a little more work on your aim is in order?" One bushy red eyebrow lifted at her.

"A worthy goal? Really? Thanks! " she said, stunned by the unexpected compliment. If it *was* a compliment. She wasn't absolutely sure. "Oh, and I'll work on that aim part," she added.

In truth she was surprised and thrilled that he'd noticed her rainbow-making skills at all. But maybe noticing things was what made him such an effective principal. And made him someone from whom it would be dangerous to keep a secret, she thought, remembering Hera's letterscroll in her bag. Which was front and center on her lap right now. Oh, why hadn't she thought to tuck her bag under her chair when she'd sat down!

Zeus opened his mouth to continue on, probably to lecture her about the dangers of arcing rainbows at principals who have lightning-fast tempers and thunderbolt weapons.

To head him off she spoke first again. "Actually, I've been wanting to talk to you about my rainbows." As she said the words, she started to ease her bag to one side of her lap, hoping to slip it onto the floor beneath her chair.

Unfortunately, that only drew his attention to it. And when Iris looked down, she was horrified to see that Hera's scroll had slid halfway out of her bag. Zeus had spotted it too, and his gaze was now fixed on the name written on the outside of it.

"That looks like Hera's handwriting." His blue eyes narrowed. "Who's Ceyx?"

Iris pressed back in her chair. "Oh. Um, yes, this is a message that I'm taking to the IM for Hera. I don't know who Ceyx is, though." The truth was best, right? After all, she wasn't doing anything wrong.

Tiny sparks of electricity started prickling all along the principal's muscled arms. Sure signs that he was annoyed. The uneasy way Iris was acting had made him suspicious!

"You can give Hera's letterscroll to me," he said in a sly tone of voice. "I'll deliver it for her." He half-rose from his seat, reaching for it.

Quickly Iris tucked her bag with the scroll inside it all the way under her chair. She couldn't believe she'd done that! But she took secrets seriously, and messages written in letterscrolls were secrets, in her opinion. Though she knew she might get fried for her daring, she sat up tall and said, "This message was entrusted to me, so *I'll* deliver it."

Appearing taken aback, Zeus plopped into his throne again. He seemed to study her with a new respect. Then he stroked his red beard and said, "I can see you are an exceptionally trustworthy student." His eyes slid to the map on his desk for a second. Then he looked at her again, as if sizing her up some more. "I have an appointment in a few minutes. And while I'm away, there's a special mission that I can only give to someone trustworthy. Are you up for it?"

Iris straightened, pleased. Zeus trusted her! She wondered if the mission would involve rainbows. Could it be a test of some kind to see how well she was able to handle messages and secrets? Maybe he wanted her to take a message to the Gray Ladies! Regardless, she would handle whatever it was and prove herself worthy of his trust.

"Sure. What is it? You can count on me," she replied eagerly.

"Good. I want you to fetch something for me, Isis."

"Iris," she corrected. "Isis is an Egyptian goddess." Like everyone else at MOA, she knew this because a while back Aphrodite had publicly tangled with Isis over which of them was the real goddess of love.

"The item you must fetch is a pitcher of water," Zeus was saying, seeming not to have heard the part about getting her name wrong. "And don't spill a drop of it on the way back to my office."

Zeus had called her here because he was thirsty? Whatever! At least he didn't seem to be planning to zap her.

"Okay," said Iris. "I have a very good sense of balance

and am not at all clumsy. I should be able to manage a pitcher of water without spilling it." She grabbed her bag and hopped up to head for the door. The water fountains at MOA were all filled with sparkling nectar, but there would be plenty of water and pitchers in the cafeteria kitchen for cooking. Maybe if she fulfilled this easy-peasy mission for him, he'd look favorably upon her request to become the official Goddess of Rainbows!

"Wait! Sit!" Zeus thundered.

Iris sat.

"This is no ordinary pitcher I'm requesting. It's a special one. With unusual powers I think will help solve a certain . . . looming situation. I heard a rumor that it has been spotted in a store called Ship Shape in the Immortal Marketplace. I don't know exactly what it looks like, but you'll know it because it's the only pitcher in the store."

"Yes, sir. I'm on it!" Iris declared.

Zeus grinned a little at her enthusiastic reply, but then grew serious again. "Be careful with it. And tell no one else what's been said on your visit here today."

Iris nodded. He seemed ready for her to leave, but she was still full of questions. What was the importance of this pitcher? And why were he and Hera both being so secretive all of a sudden? Was Iris also supposed to keep secret what she'd overheard about Typhon earlier?

She was about to ask, when Ms. Hydra hollered to Zeus from somewhere in the vicinity of his office doorway. "Hera's waiting in the courtyard. Time to go!"

Zeus jumped up. Standing, he was even more impressive and intimidating than when sitting. Because he was seven feet tall! He ran to the window. From what she could see from where she sat, the sky had grown dark and stormy in the distance. Was that Typhon's doing? Zeus came back to his desk and haphazardly rolled up the map to the Gray Ladies' office. As he clenched it in one meaty fist, his intense eyes narrowed on her again.

"Take heed." He pointed to a scorched sign on his wall that was hanging precariously from a single nail at one corner. It read: WHAT YOU HEAR IN ZEUS'S OFFICE STAYS IN ZEUS'S OFFICE.

Then, without another word, he dashed off. A half second later Ms. Hydra came along and ushered Iris out of his office.

Outside on the front steps of the Academy, Iris found Antheia waiting for her with two mortal girls. One had golden hair streaked with blue. Her bangs were in the shape of question marks, signifying that she was the most curious girl in school—Pandora. The other girl had snakes instead of hair growing from her head—Medusa.

Antheia had just finished weaving a bunch of little

flower wreaths. A dozen, in fact. Each was the size of a baby's bracelet. "There you go," she said, handing them to Medusa, who grinned at her in thanks.

"Ooh! Aren't they cute?" cooed Pandora. The two mortal girls stood to go. Out in the courtyard, custodians were already arriving to clean up the mess the winds had made, but some things, such as broken statues, would have to be replaced.

As the girls moved off, Medusa began calling out her snakes' names one by one. "Viper, Flicka, Pretzel, Snapper, Twister, Slinky, Lasso, Slither, Scaly, Emerald, Sweetpea, Wiggle." As she pronounced each snake's name, it bowed in turn, and Pandora helped her slip a little wreath onto its head.

Just as Iris sat down on the step beside Antheia, Zeus passed overhead on the winged Pegasus. And right alongside him Hera rode in an elegant one-seater chariot pulled by magic flying peacocks.

"How'd it go?" Antheia asked. "Did you ask him about–"

"Being named the official Goddess of Rainbows?" Iris shook her head. "Nuh-uh. Not yet. Wasn't the right time." Then she grinned to lighten the mood. "But at least I didn't get zapped!"

Typhon, the pitcher mission, Hera's secret scroll. So many things were still swirling around in her head as she watched Zeus, Hera, and Pegasus disappear into the distance.

As she began taking off her sandals, she looked at her BFF. "Still up for going to the IM?"

When Antheia nodded, Iris handed her one of the two pairs of winged sandals she'd picked up from the big basket just inside the front doors of the Academy. They set their regular sandals to one side of the steps, then stood and slipped the winged sandals on to make the trip to the Immortal Marketplace. The sandals laced themselves up and the silver wings at their heels began to flap. Immediately the girls rose to hover a few inches above the ground. They leaned slightly forward. Then they were off, gliding smoothly over the courtyard, then down Mount Olympus.

Whoosh! Halfway to the IM, a big gust of wind rocked them, making them lose their balance. They clutched at one another to keep from falling. Antheia pointed upward. "Look! It's two of those wind-brothers!"

Iris looked up to see Boreas and Zephyr about twenty feet above them and flying much faster. Those godboys didn't need winged sandals. They had their own wings at their backs plus their winds to keep them aloft.

She cupped a hand around her mouth. "Stop it!" she called. "You're making us wobble!"

Leaning over, Zephyr said something to Boreas. Instantly the winds died down as the pair of them rose to join their other two brothers, who were even higher in the sky. All four boys whisked off ahead of the girls.

"I hope they aren't going to the IM too," said Antheia as the girls flew on.

"Or if they are, I hope we don't run into them there," added Iris. She and Antheia had important business to attend to. They couldn't afford to have that band of windy brothers messing things up for them!

4

Ship Shape

IRIS AND ANTHEIA EVENTUALLY REACHED THE Immortal Marketplace, touching down at its entrance. After loosening the straps around their ankles, they tied them around their sandals' silver wings to hold them in place so they could walk at a normal speed.

The IM was enormous, with a beautiful high-ceilinged roof made of crystal. Once inside, the two goddessgirls walked past rows of tall columns that separated the various shops, until they reached the center atrium. They rounded the splashing fountain and the magical rhododendron bushes that encircled it and bloomed with flowers all year round.

"No sign of those winds," said Antheia, craning to look in all directions.

"Good. Maybe those rainbow wreckers were going to Earth instead," Iris replied.

Moving on, they approached the fantastic carousel that MOA students had recently helped construct in the marketplace. It featured life-size rides of their favorite animals. All were brightly painted, had one or more seats, and were big enough so anyone could comfortably ride them as the carousel turned. Dionysus had built a leopard ride. Aphrodite had made a copy of the swan cart she possessed that really flew. There was a milk-white deer with golden antlers, like the deer that guided

Artemis's chariot. And Poseidon had made a dolphin ride. Athena had even created a replica of her Trojan horse that had helped win the Trojan War!

Instead of creating a ride, Iris and Persephone had decorated the carousel itself, adding radiant rainbows (Iris's idea) and cute kittens and flowers (Persephone's idea), as well as touches of shiny gold and swirls of color.

Just beyond the carousel, Iris pushed open the door to the shop Cassandra's family owned. The sign in its front window read: ORACLE-O BAKERY AND SCROLLBOOKS.

Inside the shop both girls sniffed the air. It was filled with the warm, sweet smells of cinnamon and sugar. "Mmm," they said at the same time.

"Something smells *heavenly*!" added Iris.

"That's an appropriate description. It's freshly made divinity fortune cookies!" said a cheerful voice. They turned to see Princess Cassandra of Troy coming into the bakery side of the shop from the scrollbook side. Her fire-gold hair was caught up in a dainty clasp, and she was wearing star-and-moon earrings.

She picked up a tray of divinity from the counter and held it out, waving it under their noses. "Want some? Free samples. They have paper fortunes in them, though, not the spoken kind you usually get at MOA."

"Sure, thanks!" Iris took one. She hadn't had lunch yet and accepted the cookie gratefully. When Antheia hesitated, Iris gently elbowed her in the ribs. Just because Apollo liked Cassandra was no reason to be rude to her and refuse her cookies!

After Antheia accepted one, Iris told the princess, "Oh, and I have something for you, too." She pulled Apollo's scroll from her bag and handed it over.

Looking excited, Cassandra set down her tray and unrolled the letterscroll on the glass countertop. "Oh, how sweet," she murmured. "We have a school holiday next Friday, and Apollo invited me to go with him to visit some of my family in Troy. He's so thoughtful!" She studied the letterscroll more closely. "These decorations around the border are really cute. I wonder who did them."

"Iris," Antheia informed her curtly.

"Glad you like them," Iris told Cassandra in a friendly voice that she hoped would cover Antheia's less-than-friendly tone. She pulled the fortune from her cookie, then saw with surprise that there were two slips of paper instead of only one.

"You got a double fortune," Cassandra told Iris, clapping her hands together and looking pleased. "That's extra lucky."

Iris scanned the writing on both fortunes. "Hmm. Are these your Opposite Oracle-O ones? The kind where I'm supposed to believe the opposite of what the fortune says?"

Opposite Oracle-Os were Cassandra's very own line of cookies. The princess couldn't foretell truth in her fortunes because of an old irreversible curse Apollo had accidentally put on her that caused her fortunes to come out all wrong. However, she and Athena had come up with a brilliant solution to fix things. You just had to believe the opposite of the fortune you got in her cookies, because that was what would actually come true!

"Yes, these are Opposite Oracle-Os," said Cassandra. "Why?"

Iris read her fortunes aloud. "Because my first one says: 'You will not find trouble,' which means I *will* find trouble. The second one is better, though, I guess. It says: 'You will not find a new crush.'

"Oh. Well, sorry about the trouble, but the new crush part could be nice, right?" said Cassandra.

"I only got one fortune, but it's the same as Iris's second one: 'You will not find a new crush,' Antheia said. "Thing is, I don't *want* to find a new crush. I'm happy with the one I have." She eyed Cassandra suspiciously as if she believed the princess had given her this fortune on purpose to make her stop crushing on Apollo.

Cassandra didn't react, however. She probably had no clue that Antheia even *liked* Apollo. Antheia really needed to give up on him, Iris thought with an inward sigh. But despite all evidence to the contrary, her friend seemed certain he'd fall in like with her one day.

"Do you know someone named Ceyx?" Iris asked Cassandra now, hoping to head off an uncomfortable topic of conversation.

"Sure, he and Alcyone—that's his wife—own a store in

the IM called Ship Shape," she answered as she wrote a message back to Apollo. After handing her letterscroll reply to Iris to give to him, she pointed to the end of the IM opposite the entrance the two girls had come in.

"Ship Shape? That's a—" Iris had started to say "coincidence." Because it *was* a coincidence that the person Hera's scroll was for was the exact same person who owned the shop where Zeus wanted her to find that pitcher. But then she remembered that her mission was a secret one. "—a big help. Thanks!" she finished instead.

Iris stuck Cassandra's reply-scroll into her bag beside Hera's letterscroll for Ceyx, and the two goddessgirls headed off toward where Cassandra had directed them. Along the way Iris oohed and aahed over the window displays in various shops, hoping to entice Antheia into stopping at one of them. That way she could go on alone to deliver Hera's message and take care of her secret errand for Zeus at the Ship Shape store. She only hoped that the pitcher, when she found it, would fit inside her bag—and be watertight—so that she could keep it hidden from Antheia!

As the two girls came even with Arachne's Sewing Supplies, Iris pointed out some shiny lengths of colored ribbons in the window that would look great woven into Antheia's wreaths. No luck. At Cleo's Cosmetics they waved to Cleo, the purple-haired, three-eyed makeup lady at the counter. "Ooh, that shade of lip gloss would look amazing on you," Iris cooed, pointing to a display in the front window. "Why don't you go in and—"

"Those fortunes were so lame," Antheia grumbled, interrupting her.

Iris stared at her friend in surprise. She couldn't

believe Antheia was still brooding about those silly scraps of paper!

"Good luck?" Antheia scoffed as the girls walked on. "I don't think so. That double fortune you got only shows how careless Cassandra was in making them. I think she accidentally put two fortunes in the same cookie, is all!"

"Mm-hm," said Iris. She refused to go along with Antheia's grumpiness, which she figured was only inspired by jealousy. In fact, Antheia's aura was pale green right now, which indicated that emotion. As they drew closer to their destination, Iris began to fear that her BFF would *never* take the hint and let her go to Ship Shape alone.

Then suddenly Antheia cried out, "Oh! Look how cute!" She stopped to gaze longingly at the plants in the window of Demeter's Daisies, Daffodils, and Floral Delights. It was Persephone's mom's shop. Though Persephone was into flowers in a big way like her mom and had the greenest thumb at MOA, Antheia's thumb was a close second. Except she was more about using flowers, ferns, berries, nuts, and other vegetation to create wreaths for every occasion.

Iris nudged her with an elbow. "Go on in. While you shop, I'll take Hera's scroll to Ceyx at that Ship Shape shop Cassandra told us about. You can meet me there when you're ready."

"Okay," Antheia agreed, going inside the store.

Phew! Iris hurried off to find Ceyx. She needed to deliver Hera's letterscroll and look for that pitcher. Fast—before Antheia caught up with her and Iris had to explain things Zeus didn't want her to explain. Luckily, after passing a shop called Magical Wagical, she spotted a blue door marked SHIP SHAPE.

Pushing through the door, she found herself standing on a gangplank that rested on pontoons atop a big pool of water. To her surprise, the whole inside of the shop was a freshwater lake!

"Whoa!" She grabbed the handrails on either side of her, which were nothing more than thick ropes looped between a series of waist-high poles all along the walkway. There were all kinds of fish frolicking around in the lake, and birds flying through the air. An open skylight in the ceiling allowed the birds to fly in and out of the shop. And floating out in the middle of the lake, at the far end of the gangplank, was a wooden sailing ship!

Deciding that that must be the actual store part of the shop, Iris held the thick rope handrail and walked across the bouncy gangplank until she reached the ship's entrance. She had to stoop and duck through the small open hatch door because it was a few inches too short for her. The walls inside the shop were lined with shelves stocked with bags of birdseed, boxes of fish food, and various pet toys and medicines. Apparently it was a pet supply store, mostly selling stuff for birds and fish.

"Hello?" she called. "Ceyx? Alcyone?" No answer. And she didn't see anything even resembling a pitcher on any of the shelves either.

As Iris stood there wondering what to do, two small birds swooped in to land on a counter at the far side of the store. Both had bright blue-green wings and heads, orange-feathered bellies, and red feet. Their beaks were extra long and pointy, and they were chattering and tweeting away to each other. Suddenly they switched from bird talk to human speech.

"Zeus, tweety, did you remember to order the

parrot food?" asked the slightly smaller bird.

"Yes, Hera, my tweetheart, I did," said the larger bird. Then it pecked at its feathers, preening.

Iris couldn't help it. She giggled. She couldn't believe that the birds were named Zeus and Hera. And what they'd said was just sooo weird!

At the sound of her giggle, the two birds squawked in alarm and instantly shapeshifted into normal-size mortals, a man and a woman. Each wore an orange-feathered tunic and had blue-green hair that stood up in a straight fan that went from the forehead to the back of the neck, like a Mohawk haircut.

"May I help you?" asked the man. Tilting his head sideways, he looked at her through one eye.

"Are you the shopkeepers?" asked Iris. "My name is Iris. I go to Mount Olympus Academy. I'm here looking for someone named Ceyx?"

"That's me," said the man. After tilting his head in the opposite direction so that he could look at her through his other eye, he hopped forward in birdlike fashion. "Ceyx Kingfisher's the name."

"And I'm Alcyone," said his wife, tilting her head this way and that as well.

"But why were you calling each other Zeus and Hera?" Iris cocked her head in confusion, then quickly straightened it, realizing she'd been unconsciously imitating the way these two birds—er, shape-shifting mortals were moving their heads in quick tilts and turns.

"Oh," Ceyx said sheepishly. "Those are just our pet names for each other."

Alcyone nodded her head in a series of little jerks. "Everyone talks about how happy Zeus and Hera are. So in love. Like us!" She shared a happy smile with Ceyx.

Iris could see by their sunny yellow auras that what

they said was true. They were as happy as lovebirds!

"You can call us by our real names, though," Ceyx said quickly. "We use the pet names only with each other. It's meant as a compliment to the gods," he declared.

Iris wasn't so sure Zeus would see it that way if he got wind of this. He could be touchy about certain things, and this pair of birds using his and Hera's names as nicknames was probably one of them.

"Well, Hera asked me to give this to you," Iris said. She pulled the letterscroll from her bag and handed it to Ceyx.

He gave Alcyone a confused look as he took the letterscroll. "What's up with the delivery service? Couldn't you have just given this to me yourself?"

"I've never seen that scroll in my life!" exclaimed Alcyone with another quick jerk of her head.

"No! It's from the *real* Hera," Iris explained.

"Oh, that makes more sense," said Ceyx. "Why didn't you say so?" He unrolled it on the counter and began reading with his left eye.

"Snack?" Alcyone offered. Iris turned to see that she was holding out a bowl filled with birdseed.

"No, thanks," said Iris. "I'm not hungry." Unfortunately, her stomach chose just that moment to grumble. She hoped Alcyone hadn't heard. Although Iris was actually starving, she didn't want to eat birdseed. But she also didn't want to hurt the bird-lady's feelings.

"This is terrible!" Ceyx warbled in an alarmed voice, drawing their attention. His head bobbed up and down as he tapped a finger on the letterscroll Iris had delivered. "It's a warning from Hera. She heard about our pet names and says if Zeus finds out, he'll be mighty angry. She thinks he might mistakenly think I'm trying to impersonate him. Or decide I have a crush on Hera—his wife, that is."

"Oh no! What are we going to do?" squawked Alcyone, drowning out Iris's shocked gasp.

"Let's get our names officially changed to 'Hera' and 'Zeus,'" suggested Ceyx. "That way Zeus won't be mad if he finds out."

"Good plan, tweety pie!" said Alcyone.

Huh? thought Iris. These two were birdbrains if they thought that would work! "Or maybe you could write to Hera and promise not to use the pet names anymore," she suggested.

"Even better!" said Alcyone.

"And a lot less paperwork." Ceyx got out a blank letterscroll and quickly penned a reply to Hera, then handed it to Iris. "Will you deliver it?"

"Sure," said Iris. She'd be glad to help head off trouble!

"Hurry off now. Fly away," said Alcyone, making a flapping motion toward Iris with her arms.

Just then Iris glimpsed Antheia coming up the gangplank toward the ship. Iris couldn't let her find out about the pitcher. "One more thing, though," she told the bird-mortals in a rush. "I also came for a pitcher. A special one that Zeus wants."

"I only remember having one pitcher. That fancy one with the stopper that we got from those pickers," said Ceyx.

"We should've known better than to buy anything from those Harpies," said Alcyone. "They fool us every time."

Iris groaned silently. Her Harpy sisters, Alcyone meant. Though they owned and operated the café here in the IM, they still liked to roam the heavens and Earth in their spare time, searching for interesting items to pick up and resell. Hence the nickname: pickers. Only, more often than not they *picked up* items that already belonged to someone else! *Stole* them, in other words.

"Right. I remember. We traded feather-combs to them for it," said Ceyx.

"Can I have it?" Iris asked eagerly.

Alcyone shook her head. "We gave the pitcher to the Goddess Styx earlier today. She came in for fish food and saw it. Apparently it had been stolen from her."

Iris's eyes went wide. "The Goddess Styx? As in the one who guards the River Styx? The boundary between Earth and the Underworld?"

The big birds both nodded.

"Since the pitcher was stolen goods," Ceyx went on, "we had to return it to her."

Oh no! thought Iris. The Underworld was not only dank and dark; it was scary and maybe a little dangerous. Like most MOA students, she had never set foot there. And she never wanted to either! A student named Hades, who seemed kind of gloomy to her, was the godboy of the Underworld. And he was constantly warning others to stay away from the place.

"Hi! What did I miss?" asked Antheia, poking her head in through the doorway.

"Nothing," Iris, Ceyx, and Alcyone all said at the same time.

5

Hungry, Hungry Harpies

IRIS PAUSED TO GAZE AT THE MAGICAL GIFTS IN A gift store window as she and Antheia headed back through the IM. She was also thinking hard, giving herself time to figure out what to do about the pitcher. In the window were artfully arranged decorations, including papyrus-tissue wedding bells and big white gift boxes with elaborate bows.

"That's pretty," said Antheia, pointing out a silver tea

set. The second she spoke, the lid on the decorative box nearest to the tea set lifted, and a puppet popped out like a jack-in-the-gift-box. It wore a white tunic with a formal black bowtie at its neck.

Staring at window decorations wasn't going to help Iris decide whether she should go to the Underworld this afternoon to try to find the Goddess Styx. If she went, it might be dark by the time she got there. Where did the Goddess Styx live anyway? Probably somewhere along the long, winding, sludgy Styx River that bordered the Underworld. She shuddered at the very idea of making such a visit. Still, she didn't want to let Zeus down.

Becoming aware that the puppet in the window had sprung toward them and was waiting for her or Antheia to ask a question about one of the gifts on display, she told it, "We're just window shopping." Looking a little disappointed, the puppet sank back down into its box, and the lid closed over the top of it again.

"What's wrong?" Antheia asked her as they moved on. "I can tell you're upset. What happened with Ceyx? What did Hera's letterscroll say?"

"Well," Iris began, shooting her an uncertain glance. She really didn't want to get into it, since telling a little information would lead to questions about stuff Zeus had asked her not to reveal.

"Hey!" someone called out before Iris could go on. The girls looked over their shoulders to see Zephyr coming their way. No wild winds swirled around him now, not even a breeze.

"You're that girl from MOA. Iris, right?" Zephyr said to her. "The one with the pens and the Harpy sisters? I saw you in Zeus's office."

Iris sucked in a sharp breath. "No! I mean, yes, I'm

Iris. And my sisters are Harpies, but I'm not." She was glad for a chance to tell him, and she hoped he'd tell his brothers. She loved her older sisters, but the three of them had a bad reputation for thieving and driving people crazy. They even drove *her* crazy most of the time, and she was always trying to keep their reputation from rubbing off on her.

"Well, I saw you from the window of their café and just wanted to warn you that they're stirring up trouble in there. "

Stirring up trouble? He was one to talk. She knew that her three sisters weren't perfect–not even close. But his three brothers weren't exactly well-behaved either! Especially that Boreas. "What kind of trouble? Not a food fight, I hope."

"Not yet, but they've been stealing–um, borrowing from their own customers and–"

“Oh no!” Having spent plenty of time in the Hungry, Hungry Harpy Café her sisters owned, Iris could well imagine the rest. She spun around and took off down the mall, with Antheia and Zephyr right behind her. Seconds later she was grabbing the pair of H-shaped door handles and pushing into the café.

It was filled with secondhand items the Harpies had handpicked or, at least in the case of the smallest items, pick-*pocketed* over the years. They proudly used stolen goods as decorations, and the café walls were covered with them. The ceilings, too. There was an antique violin, some rusty farm equipment, paper fans, sparkly costume jewelry, and even a few items supposedly once owned by immortals.

Two dozen or so back issues of *Teen Scrollazine* and the *Greekly Weekly News* had been framed and hung on the wall behind the order counter. The issues had been selected based on how important, wild, or amusing their headlines were. For instance: ZEUS TO WED HERA! And SUN CHARIOT CRASHES, CAUSING FIRE! Plus, TROUBLE BUBBLES WREAK HAVOC AT MOA!

Almost immediately Iris saw what had gotten Zephyr so worried. A gray-haired mortal man was sitting at the counter on a stool made from an old leather trunk. There was an angry look on his face, and he held on tight to his silverware, as if afraid his utensils might be snatched away. He had a right to be worried!

Because Iris's three Harpy sisters—Aello, Celaeno, and Ocypete—were all standing nearby, watching him intently. Their faces bore a resemblance to Iris's. But their wings were huge and enabled them to fly, unlike her more delicate ones.

As Iris headed for the counter, the gray-haired man slammed his fist down on it, denting it a little. (There were already many such dents in the counter from other dissatisfied customers.) "That's the second blue-plate special you've stolen from under my nose," the man yelled at the Harpies. "What have you done with it? Give it back!"

"Now, Phineas, you're mistaken," cooed Aello.

Meanwhile, Celaeno skillfully swiped his napkin when he wasn't looking. "We gave you those blue-plate specials and you ate them. You just don't remember."

"It wouldn't be fair to ask for another," added Ocypete. "Unless you want to pay for a third one."

"What? I will *not* pay for a third, and I want you to return my money for the first two you stole." As he was arguing with Ocypete, Aello sneaked up from behind him and snitched his glass of tea, quickly drank it, and then set the glass back down before he noticed.

Phineas reached for his glass seconds later, and

became angry when he found it empty. "Hey! Where's my tea?"

"Crazy kleptomaniacs," muttered Boreas. He was sitting in a booth with Notus and Eurus, near enough for Iris to hear. Zephyr and Antheia were over by them too.

Iris glared at Boreas. He was right, though. Her sisters were up to their usual tricks—stealing food from customers as fast as they served it to them. As Phineas stood to go, Celaeno wrote out a bill and handed it to him.

He wadded it up and threw it over his shoulder, shouting, "I told you. I'm not going to pay for food I didn't eat!"

As Zephyr had suspected, a fight was brewing.

"Don't worry. I'll take care of this!" Iris called to Phineas. She usually spent her summers working here in the café, so she knew how to handle the trouble her Harpy sisters caused. Smiling brightly, she dashed back to the kitchen. When she reappeared, she handed him a to-go dinner in a see-through box. "Here you go, sir. One blue-plate special. On the house."

"He has to pay for that," Aello said in outrage.

"That's too big of a helping," Celaeno insisted.

"Let us just have a taste of it to be sure it's okay," said Ocypete, reaching for the box.

Ignoring them, Iris ushered Phineas and his box out of the café. "Thank you! Come again!" she called after him.

Once he was gone, she turned back to see that all the remaining customers in the café were gaping at her and her sisters. As always, such looks made her want to sink into the floor. Her older sisters were just sooo embarrassing!

Iris opened her mouth to scold them for about the thousandth time in her life, but stopped when her eyes fell on a set of boy's baby clothes that had been framed like a picture and hung on the café wall. How strange! She looked more closely and gasped in surprise. Those weren't just any old baby clothes. The label claimed that Zeus had worn the little tunic when he was six months old! Supposedly. It *did* have scorch marks on it. Still, you never knew with her sisters whether an item was the genuine thing or not.

"Into the kitchen," Iris ordered the Harpy trio. Obediently they trooped into the kitchen, and she followed. Honestly, sometimes she felt like the older sister in this bunch.

"Did you steal a pitcher from the Goddess Styx?" she asked them. She didn't bother scolding them about their treatment of customers. She'd tried that too many times before to no avail.

Her sisters appeared insulted by her question. "Steal?" echoed Aello.

"We've never stolen anything in our lives," huffed Celaeno. "We merely pick up lost things and give them a home." She always attempted to paint their bad behavior in the best possible light.

"You always blame us, Little Sister," Ocypete added as she opened the oven and pulled something from it that smelled delicious. "So unfair. However, since you mention it, we did borrow such a pitcher from the Goddess Styx and lend it to Ceyx."

Before Iris could question them further, Aello glanced at something beyond her and said, "Is that your boyfriend?"

"What?" Iris looked over her shoulder to see Zephyr craning his head toward the kitchen from where he sat at the table with his brothers. To her surprise Antheia was sitting with them too, talking with the boys she'd claimed were so annoying.

Catching Iris's eye, Zephyr appeared ready to come to her assistance if she beckoned. She shook her head at him. She could handle this.

"He's *not* my boyfriend," she told her sisters. Good thing she didn't blush easily. And supergood thing that she was the only person she knew who could read auras. Hers was probably the shade of deep red that meant major embarrassment right now.

"Why don't you go have a seat with your not-boyfriend, then," Celaeno teased, ushering her out of the kitchen. "And we'll serve you all a nice lunch."

"Uh. Okay. Thanks," said Iris. The delicious smells of the food cooking in pots and pans all around her were practically making her dizzy. She was starving! She figured the birds' scroll could wait just a little longer to be delivered to Hera. At least she hoped so. "But please, don't you dare steal back any of the food you serve us, okay?"

"Of course not!" her three sisters exclaimed innocently.

Rolling her eyes, Iris went over to the booth where the others were, and her sisters immediately served them all blue-plate specials. She wound up sitting by Zephyr. Antheia was across from her between Boreas and Eurus.

Iris knew her sisters had kept her from scolding them by offering lunch and teasing her about Zephyr being her boyfriend. Typical! They were tricky like that. They had bad manners and cackled, burped, and flapped their wings as they pleased. And despite their repeated promises not to steal things, they always did. So was it any wonder they were such an embarrassment to her?

Still, she wasn't happy when Boreas began to make fun of them as soon as she sat down. "So what's it like having food-rustling soup-snatchers for sisters?" he asked her.

"Nobody's perfect," she snapped as she dug into the tasty meal. "And don't forget that they made this food we're eating and gave us a place to sit and eat it. I assume you must like it here, or you'd go somewhere else!"

"Ooh! Burned me!" Boreas replied, laughing as if he didn't take the whole thing seriously at all. Still smiling his smirky smile, he began teasing Antheia instead.

"So was that your rainbow we saw this morning when we flew over the sports fields? I mean, you make rainbows?" Zephyr asked her a minute later.

Iris nodded, keeping a close eye on the Harpies as they came and went. When Ocypete tried to nab the saltshaker from the table, Iris cleared her throat and shook her head at her. Ocypete grinned and set the shaker back down. Stealing was like a game to those sisters of hers!

"Awesome. How do you do it?" asked Zephyr.

"Do what?" Iris asked blankly. Then she realized he

must still have been talking about her rainbows, and she shrugged. “That’s like me asking you how you and your brothers make the winds blow. You can just do it, right?”

“Right, but there’s a science behind what we do,” he said. Sipping his tea, he explained. “Basically, the sun heats the Earth unevenly, causing warm air and cool air. Warm air weighs less than cool air so it rises. Cool air sinks. My brothers and I take that air movement and give it speed and direction. As simple as that.”

Iris laughed. “Simple, huh? I don’t think so.” He seemed as fascinated by weather as she was. To her surprise this boy was turning out to be kind of interesting!

He grinned back and gave his head a toss, flipping the chestnut-brown hair from his sky-blue eyes. Which she’d just noticed had soft gray flecks in them. “So, what about rainbows? There must be some trick to them,” he insisted.

No one had ever asked her that before, but now Iris considered it. "Well, I guess what happens is that I make thin beams of light stream from my fingers. Using magic, of course. Then I aim those light beams at really tiny droplets of water suspended high in the air. The droplets act like thousands of tiny prisms."

Just then Antheia interrupted, calling something across the table that Iris didn't quite catch. It was getting hard to hear because the three Harpies had begun singing loudly and clashing dishes as they cleared a nearby table.

"What?" Iris called back, cupping her ear.

"Pass the salt!" Antheia repeated.

As Iris reached for the saltshaker, Zephyr picked up the thread of their conversation again. "I get it. So your beams of light pass through the raindrops, which breaks them into all kinds of colors."

"Exactly," said Iris, smiling at him. "And voila! A rainbow!" To demonstrate she stuck her fingers into the bottom of her glass, where there was an inch of water. She flicked water droplets into the air over her plate and quickly shot a little rainbow to arc through them and across the table to Antheia. Then she sent the saltshaker sliding up and over the rainbow to her BFF, who caught it in her hands.

Antheia laughed, and all five of Iris's companions hooted and clapped. Even Boreas.

"It all happens really fast, so it's hard for anyone else to see what's going on," Iris went on to Zephyr. "All of a sudden a rainbow is just there."

They continued chatting about weather-related topics, and then she said, "Can I ask you something?"

He nodded.

"Principal Zeus told me not to repeat what I heard

in his office," she said. "But I figure you already know about a certain monster whose name starts with *T*?" The Harpies were now doing an impromptu flamenco dance to entertain their customers, and it had gotten so loud that Iris had to lean in toward Zephyr so he'd hear. Which was kind of good because it also meant that the others couldn't listen in.

Zephyr went on instant alert, his eyes going serious as they searched hers. "You mean Typhon? Does anyone else know?" He flicked a concerned glance at Antheia.

Iris shook her head. "No. But how worried should I be for MOA?"

Since Antheia couldn't overhear from across the table, Zephyr seemed to decide he could safely speak. "It's pretty bad. T. is the fiercest of all creatures. An enormous tornado with winds far stronger than my own. When he stands still—which isn't often—his head touches the stars and his hands touch the east and west horizons. And two days ago he broke out of captivity in Tartarus and went on a rampage, destroying cities and hurling mountains. But now he's lying low. My brothers and I are patrolling the skies around MOA, waiting for his next move."

"You can't stop him *before* he strikes? And do you know what his plan is, by the way?" Iris's thoughts were racing now, real fear filling her.

"No. We only know that he's after Zeus," Zephyr admitted solemnly.

Iris gasped. "Why? Wait. Is it because Zeus is the one who locked him up in Tartarus?"

"Yeah, at the end of the war between the Olympian gods and the Titans. If T. defeats Zeus this time—which he won't if we have anything to say about it—we think he'll try to start a new war against all Olympians. Aimed at their total destruction." Zephyr picked up a piece of toasted bread and crumbled it to illustrate his point.

"Hey," called Boreas. "What are you talking about so secretly over there?"

"Nothing," Zephyr said calmly. Then he leaned toward Iris again. "Keep all this to yourself, okay? Zeus doesn't want anyone to panic. With his help we'll stop that beast, no problem."

Somehow she believed him. At least she believed he would try, so she nodded. Then, realizing she'd been staring at Zephyr for a while, Iris drew back. She felt her cheeks warm despite the fact that she hardly ever blushed.

"C'mon, then," Boreas said to his brother. "We're heading over to Mighty Fighty. We could need what they sell one day soon. If you know what I mean." He flicked a glance at Iris, then looked back at Zephyr as if warning him not to spill the beans about Typhon to her. Little did he know the beans had already been spilled.

When the four boys stood to leave, Iris and Antheia did as well. Mighty Fighty was a store that all the boys seemed to love. It sold spears, javelins, bows and arrows, shields, armor, and other such stuff. Iris suspected the windy brothers must be going there to get ideas on how to win a battle against Typhon.

As the girls watched the windy godboys head down the mall, Iris's gaze lingered on Zephyr. He was kind of cute and nice after all, she decided. Not like that Boreas. Zephyr seemed to be as different from him as she was from the Harpies!

Outside the IM, Iris and Antheia loosened the ties on their sandals to free the silver wings at their heels. The ties twined around their ankles again, and the silver wings began to flap. In seconds their sandals whisked them up the mountainside and through the clouds toward Mount Olympus Academy. On the way both goddessgirls were quiet, thinking their own thoughts.

As they arrived, a strong wind swept over them, then Zephyr and his brothers landed in the courtyard up ahead. Even though the wind-boys had left the IM later, after going to Mighty Fighty, their winds had carried them here faster than the girls' winged sandals.

For some reason Boreas practically got whiplash looking back at them, Iris noticed. Wait a second, not at *them*, she realized, tracking his gaze. Only Antheia! Come to think of it, he *had* seemed rather mesmerized by Antheia at lunch. And whenever one of his brothers had talked to her, his aura had turned a little green, as in jealous.

Hmm. Interesting. Was it possible that cold winter wind-boy liked Iris's springtime flowery friend? If Antheia ever wound up crushing back, Aphrodite would probably say it was a case of opposites attracting. Sort of like gloomy Hades and sunny Persephone, come to think of it. Or Aphrodite, the goddess of love herself, and her crush, Ares, who was the godboy of war.

"So what was Boreas saying to you at lunch?" Iris asked Antheia as their winged sandals whisked them closer to the Academy. She wasn't sure she wanted to get any kind of crush going between that blowhard boy and her best bud.

"Boreas the bore? I didn't really pay attention. I gave him the cold shoulder." Antheia laughed. "Get it?"

Iris smiled. "Yeah, I get it." She couldn't exactly blame her friend for treating him coolly. Boreas had been kind of mean to them so far.

"What were Zephyr and you talking about? What's he like?" Antheia asked as they touched down in the courtyard.

"Seems pretty nice, actually. And he's interested in weather and science." Iris gazed off into space. "Cute, too," she said dreamily.

"Yeah?" said Antheia, showing a flicker of interest. Though she hadn't paid him any attention until just that moment, her eyes fixed on Zephyr now as the boys zoomed into the school ahead of them. "Yeah, I was just thinking the same thing," she said quickly.

As the two girls sat on the steps to switch back to their walking sandals, Iris spotted Apollo in the courtyard.

She nudged Antheia and nodded toward Apollo. "I have something to do right now. Want to take this to him?" She pulled Cassandra's letterscroll out of her bag and held it out to her friend. "Cassandra entrusted it to both of us, so I don't think she'd mind."

Antheia shrugged. Surprisingly, she didn't seem as enthusiastic about the idea as Iris would've expected. "I suppose." She took the letterscroll and went to hand it to him.

Iris started up to the front doors of the Academy. Zeus was probably expecting her to deliver the pitcher to him right away. For the second time that day, she approached his office warily, sure he'd be disappointed that she hadn't gotten what he'd requested. However, when she arrived, there was a sign on the main office door. It read:

Principal Zeus is out till Monday.

None of your business where he is.

P.S. Hera is out till then too.

Must have been written by Ms. Hydra's grumpy green head, Iris decided. Still, she was relieved not to have to face the principal yet. On the way to the marble staircase, she ran into Antheia. The girl was uncharacteristically quiet as they took the stairs up to the room they shared on the fourth floor. Had something happened with Apollo? Iris didn't want to ask.

She had enough on her mind. She'd promised Zeus she'd get the pitcher, and she didn't want to let him down. She couldn't. Not if she wanted his support in becoming the rainbow goddessgirl. But did she dare go by herself to the Underworld? *Yikes!*

All the rest of that afternoon and during dinner, she waffled on a decision. She still hadn't made up her mind by that night. Iris found herself thinking about Zephyr as she and Antheia changed into their pj's, doused the candles on their desks, and climbed into their beds on opposite sides of the room.

A small smile stole over Iris's face as she snuggled under the covers. She felt the beginnings of a crush stirring and held the secret tight, enjoying being the only one who knew for now.

"Hey, Iris?" Antheia said after a few minutes had gone by.

Iris yawned. "Yeah?" she asked in a sleepy voice.

"I think I'm finally over Apollo."

"Oh?" At this news Iris perked up. Inside she was jumping for joy. Antheia's crush had been hopeless. And it had been making Antheia unhappy. Now it was over. Awesome!

"Yeah. I think I like someone else," said Antheia.

Was she crushing on Boreas? That would be a surprise, after what Antheia had said earlier. But Iris promised herself to be supportive if her friend did like him. Even though she had doubts about his crush-worthiness.

"Want to know who my new secret crush is?" Antheia asked.

Iris turned onto her side and stared at her friend through the dim room. "Well, it won't be a secret if you tell me, but . . ."

"It's Zephyr!" Antheia burst out.

"Huh?" Iris felt herself go pale. *Not again!* She and Antheia liking the same boy for a *third* time? Just like had happened with Poseidon and then Apollo? It was too much! And as before, Antheia had declared her interest in Zephyr first, before Iris had been ready to do the same. Which of course meant he would have to be off-limits to her now. It was part of the unspoken goddessgirl code. No crush stealing allowed.

"Great," Iris said weakly. But of course she meant quite the opposite. *Yeah,* she thought unhappily. *Just great.*

6

Double Crush

THE NEXT MORNING IRIS GOT UP EARLY. Antheia was still sleeping, so Iris dressed quietly in a lavender-colored chiton and matching sandals. Lavender was a shade of purple, and purple was akin to red in having properties of bravery. If she went to the Underworld today, she'd need every bit of help she could get to maintain her courage!

When she was ready, she tiptoed out of the dorm room,

clutching her bag with Ceyx's letterscroll still inside. She headed for the front office first thing, hoping Zeus and Hera were already back. Then she could deliver Ceyx's scroll to Hera if she was around, as well as talk to Zeus.

Unfortunately, the sign about them being gone from MOA was still on the main office door. Just in case they were back and Ms. Hydra had only forgotten to take the sign down, Iris opened the door and poked her head in.

"Ahem! And just what are you doing?" Ms. Hydra's grumpy green head asked.

Iris whirled around to see Zeus's nine-headed assistant standing in the hallway behind her. It was so early that Iris had beaten her to work. "I was looking for Principal Zeus."

"Can't you read?" Ms. Hydra's impatient purple head nodded toward the sign. "He and Hera have gone to an appointment. They return this afternoon."

Iris didn't bother to point out that the sign didn't specifically say "afternoon" as she watched the assistant go into the office and slither behind her desk.

Ms. Hydra's blue head, which was always sympathetic to students, craned its long serpentine neck to peer at her. "Anything I can help you with?" it asked.

"No, that's okay," Iris said, closing the door. Talking to Zeus and delivering Ceyx's reply-scroll to Hera would have to wait.

Iris's mind raced as she stood in the breakfast line in the MOA cafeteria a few minutes later. *Should I go to the Underworld before Zeus gets back?* she wondered as she took a plate of ambrosia scramble from the eight-armed lunch lady. Could she really go to such a creepy, dark, lonely, horrible place alone? A place where mortals went after they died and turned into shades? She shivered.

On the one hand, going there by herself would show

Zeus she was capable of carrying out the mission he'd given her. On the other hand, if her trip resulted in trouble, he'd be mad. Grinning to herself, she realized that if she had as many hands as the cafeteria lady, she'd have even *more* trouble deciding!

The minute she got her tray of food, she noticed Pheme darting from table to table. As usual, she was spreading some sort of news. Iris didn't have to hear her to know what she was saying. She simply read the cloud-letters that puffed from Pheme's lips and hung in the air above her.

Rumor has it they've gone to see the Gray Ladies, Pheme was saying. *To seek their advice about some sort of problem.*

Iris's brows rose. She had to be talking about Zeus and Hera. Was Pheme about to let the cat out of the windbag that this "problem" they needed help with was Typhon?

But then the gossipy girl's expression turned a bit

confused and she added, "It was something to do with communication, I think. Or maybe it was education or vacation. Anyway, some kind of problem."

Typical! thought Iris. Pheme often made mistakes in her reporting. Like the time when she'd gotten it wrong about who'd stolen the Norse goddess Freya's necklace during the Girls' Olympic Games. Remembering how mad Zeus had been about that error made Iris shudder. She wished again that she knew what he'd think about her going to the Underworld. And solo, no less.

Iris headed for the table where Antheia was sitting. Just as she arrived, a breeze blew a napkin off Iris's tray. Both girls frowned toward a nearby table. The four windy brothers were sitting there, and the breeze had come from one of them. Iris could guess who was responsible. The wind had been freezing cold.

"That Boreas is so obnoxious," said Antheia. Glaring

at him, she grabbed another napkin from a stack in the center of the table and tossed it onto Iris's tray.

In fact, her napkin wasn't the only thing to have blown off a tray. Boreas, Zephyr, Notus, and Eurus were blowing lots of stuff around to show off for Ares, Apollo, and some other godboys who'd gathered around to watch.

Antheia jumped in surprise when Iris dropped her tray hard onto the table before sitting down across from her. Iris had dropped the tray on purpose. Because she had just remembered that she was still kind of annoyed at her crush-stealing BFF. Even if Antheia had no idea that she *was* a crush stealer!

"Oops. Those trays can be slippery," Antheia said kindly. She gave Iris a big clueless smile, then looked back over at the wind-boys.

Iris felt herself soften just a little. One of the truly

cool things about Antheia was that she could always be counted on to be a loyal, encouraging friend. A true-blue friend. She would never have decided to like Zephyr if she'd known Iris liked him. At least Iris didn't *think* she would. Either way, the usually cheerful Iris couldn't quite let go of her bad mood.

After she sat down, she stabbed a fork into her ambrosia scramble. Then she yawned. Fears about the Underworld and thoughts about Antheia's crush news had kept her from sleeping well the night before.

Antheia stuck her elbow onto the table and plopped her chin into the palm of her hand, gazing at Zephyr with a silly smile on her face as she sipped nectar through a straw. He and his brothers had begun levitating their breakfast trays now in a contest to see who could hold them up in the air the longest. The MOA godboys were egging them on, and Zephyr seemed to be faring the best so far.

"He's sooo cute," Antheia cooed. And Iris didn't need to ask which of the four brothers she was talking about.

"All godboys are cute," Iris reminded her. "Almost all anyway."

"But he's sweet, too," said Antheia.

Crash! They looked over to see that Eurus had dropped the tray he'd been levitating. His three brothers' trays still held steady, though. Zephyr was even doing tricks, spinning his tray full of food and dishes around in midair. Which was a pretty cool trick, actually.

"How do you know he's sweet?" challenged Iris. "You haven't even talked to him yet."

"Well, no," Antheia admitted.

Neither one of them had really had much time to get to know Zephyr so far. Iris had just felt the beginnings of a crush herself, but now she'd have to squash those feelings because of Antheia's interest in the boy. It was so unfair!

"So, what makes you think he's sweet?" Iris insisted on knowing.

Antheia looked at her in surprise. "I can just tell. Besides, we make sense together, you know? He's the spring wind. I'm the goddess of wreaths." She looked at Iris as if expecting her to get the significance of that. Which she did not!

"Do I have to spell it out?" Antheia said with a smile when Iris only stared at her. "The spring wind spreads seeds to grow flowers and ferns and stuff, which I use in my wreaths. See? We're perfect for each other."

Iris's mouth dropped open, and she stared at Antheia even harder. "By that measure he could be perfect for Persephone, too. She's the goddess of flowers and spring."

"Whoa! Somebody's grumpy this morning," Antheia said with a frown.

"Me, you mean?" Iris took a drink of nectar. She was

hardly ever grumpy. It was just that boy trouble plus Zeus trouble plus Typhon trouble were creating her bad mood this morning.

Bang! Iris jumped. Both girls looked over at the boys to see that Notus had dropped his tray. Now only Zephyr and Boreas remained in the contest to keep their trays aloft.

When Antheia had been crushing on Apollo, she'd always seemed half-desperate and half-hopeful all the time. However, now that she'd changed crushes, she looked blissfully happy. Iris's annoyance at her bestie wavered. Maybe *she* was the one being unfair.

Yesterday, when Antheia had still liked Apollo, Iris had made a promise to herself to be supportive of Antheia's next crush. So even if it was Zephyr instead of Boreas, she should do that. After all, Antheia hadn't chosen Zephyr in order to hurt Iris or anything. It wouldn't be easy, but Iris made a solemn vow to herself right then and there that she'd back off and let Antheia like him. The same way she had earlier in the year when they'd both liked Apollo.

"Woo-hoo! Awesome!" The cheers and excitement over at the godboys' table had gotten louder. Zephyr and Boreas were competing hard to win, standing with their muscles tense now, their heads thrown back. Their gazes—one frosty white, one soft blue—were trained upward as they kept their trays aloft on the moving winds they'd created. It was a major balancing act, as the dishes atop the trays slid back and forth, threatening to spill at any moment.

"Sorry I'm grumpy. Couldn't sleep last night," Iris told Antheia, managing a weak smile. "But go on about Zephyr. I'm listening."

"Okay. Here's what I've decided. I'm not going to make the same mistake I did with Apollo, keeping quiet about my feelings for so long that he starts liking another girl," Antheia said in a firm voice. "Nuh-uh. I'm making the first move this time."

"What do you mean?"

Antheia lowered her voice and leaned forward across the table. "I'm going to send Zephyr a secret crush letter-scroll to get things going. Good idea, huh?" she said, her eyes dancing.

Iris had to admire her determination. Normally they'd both be too shy to try something like that. "What are you going to write?"

"I haven't gotten that far yet," Antheia admitted. "I guess I'll just say that he's cute, I like him, and I think he should like me back. What do you think?"

For just a fraction of a second Iris considered saying, *Yeah, sounds good.* Even though she knew a letter like that probably wouldn't get Antheia's crush off the ground. It was so curt and generic. Meaning that it didn't explain at all what was special about Zephyr.

Resolved to be helpful, Iris considered how to advise Antheia. Finally she said truthfully, "It's kind of bland. Maybe spice it up with some colorful rhyme at least?"

Antheia cocked her head, looking confused. "Huh?"

"You know, like a verse in a greeting cardscroll. Maybe: 'You are cute. I think we'd suit,'" she suggested. "Only better than that."

Antheia giggled. "Wow! That's so amazing. How did you come up with that off the top of your head?"

Iris shrugged. "You should probably say something more specific, though. Something about him."

"Like what?"

"Think about it. I'm sure you'll come up with something." Iris had finished eating by now and rose to leave.

"No way," said Antheia, grabbing her arm to stop her.

"You're the one who's good at messages and stuff. At least give me a boost in the right direction?"

Suddenly there was a huge crash. Both girls—and half the cafeteria—swung around to see that the levitation contest was over. Food spattered the boys' table and the floor around it. Boreas had won, apparently. But Zephyr was being a good sport about it. As he mock-bowed to congratulate his brother, his brown hair swung into his gray-flecked blue eyes. He flipped his head to shake his hair back, and Iris's heart squeezed at the sight. He was *sooo* cute! As she watched, he grinned at the godboys gathered around and said something that made them laugh. Then the boys all moved off.

As quick as a wink, a cafeteria lady with a long snout like an anteater was at the table nosing around the floor. *She was sucking up the spatters and crumbs! Eew!* Iris looked away.

"C'mon," Antheia begged. "You've gotta help me out."

"Okay," Iris agreed, sitting down again. She knew she would be making her suggestions a little grudgingly, though. She was Antheia's closest friend, but she wasn't perfect! "Say stuff you like about him," she coached. "How his brown hair sometimes fringes cutely over his forehead and partway over his face. And how he does that little flip of his head to move it out of his eyes." She flicked her head, demonstrating the move, then went on. "And how his eyes, by the way, are a really adorable, sparkly blue with gray flecks. And . . ."

Iris's voice trailed off as she realized she'd been suggesting all the things she'd like to have said to Zephyr herself, if their crush had ever had a chance to get off the ground.

"I just had the best idea!" Antheia gushed. "Why don't you write my secret admirer letterscroll for me? Please?" She reached into her bag, pulled out a blank letterscroll, and shoved it into Iris's hands. "You're so much better at this stuff than I am. Ooh! And sign it 'Your Secret Crush,' okay?"

As Antheia rambled on, Iris stared down at the blank letterscroll, openmouthed. This whole thing was becoming more horrible by the minute. She did *not* want to write crush notes to her own crush on another girl's behalf!

Just then Pheme zipped over to their table. Iris greeted her warmly, hoping the gossipy girl would distract Antheia long enough to make her forget about what she'd just asked Iris to do.

"Big news!" Pheme exclaimed. "I've discovered why the four winds have come to MOA!"

7

Underworld Mission

IRIS SAT UP STRAIGHTER, A LITTLE WORRIED. Once again, she feared Pheme was about to reveal the news concerning Typhon's rampage, and start a panic. Exactly what Zeus was trying to avoid. Luckily, the gossipy girl revealed an altogether different reason for the four winds' presence at MOA instead.

"Principal Zeus called the four godboys of the winds to model for a big sculpture that's going to be part of a fancy anemometer in the courtyard. Turns out it'll replace one of the statues that got broken yesterday. And, get this . . ." She paused a few seconds for dramatic effect. She was really good at delivering gossip, Iris had to admit.

"Pygmalion—the most famous sculptor on Earth—will be creating the sculpture," Pheme informed them at last. "In fact, he just arrived in the courtyard with a bunch of tools and a huge block of marble to sculpt their likenesses. Not only that—Zeus has given him magical powers to finish it in a single day!"

"Wow," said Iris.

"What's an anemometer?" Antheia asked.

Pheme scrunched up her face, looking unsure. "It has something to do with the weather. Probably to do with wind, since Zephyr and his brothers are posing for it."

"Let's ask someone who's bound to know for sure."

Iris nodded her head toward Athena, who'd finished breakfast at her usual table with Aphrodite, Persephone, and Artemis and was coming their way.

"What's an anemometer?" Pheme asked her when she got close enough to talk to.

"It's a gadget used to measure wind speed," Athena answered right away.

Of course the brainiest goddessgirl in all of MOA would know! thought Iris.

"Picture yourself holding the metal frame of an umbrella without the fabric part that keeps out the rain," Athena went on. "Attach a cup turned sideways on the end of each of the metal spokes. The hollow cups catch the wind as it flows past, which causes the long handle part to turn slowly or fast in your fist. By counting the turns of the handle over a set time period, you can calculate the average wind speed."

She set down the armload of textscrolls she was holding and picked up two empty glasses from the table. Holding them sideways, one in either hand, she spread her arms wide. Then she slowly spun in a circle to give them the idea.

"I get it," said Iris. The anemometer might be a cover for the real reason the four winds were hanging around at MOA. Still, such a device could help warn when trouble came near. Trouble with a capital *T*. As in, a monster tornado called Typhon!

"Me too," Antheia said, nodding.

"Yeah," said Pheme. "It's a thingamabobber that measures cups of wind. Got it. I can't wait to tell everyone. Thanks! Toodle-oo!" She was off again before anyone could correct her.

After she departed, Athena blinked at the other two girls. "I'm not sure she really did get it."

"You think?" joked Antheia. Then they all burst out laughing. While Antheia and Athena continued chatting, Iris noticed Persephone sitting alone at the table Athena had just come from. Aphrodite and Artemis had already finished their breakfasts and had gone to the tray return.

Abruptly deciding that she *would* go to the Underworld, Iris went over to talk to Persephone. Because if any goddessgirl at MOA knew something about that place, it was her. Since she was Hades' crush, she had visited the Underworld, where he hung out a lot.

"Hi, Persephone!" Iris said, sitting down beside her. "I'm, um, doing a report on the Underworld for extra credit in Science-ology and wondered if I could ask you some questions?" This wasn't at all true, but she had to be sneaky about getting information so as not to make Persephone suspicious. She didn't want to let Zeus down, and that included keeping the mission he'd given her a secret.

Persephone finished off the carton of nectar she'd been sipping from. "Sure, the lyrebell's not for a few minutes. Ask away."

"Well. I was wondering about the layout. There's a river around it, right? I remember some godboys hid one of Mr. Cyclops's sandals there one time, and he was hopping mad about it."

Persephone let out a little laugh. "Yeah, I remember that. His sandal was so big, they used it as a raft." She glanced around the table, as if looking for something that would help her explain the Underworld. "It would probably be easier if I drew you a map, but I don't have a—"

"Pen?" Iris had already gotten a blue one from her bag and was holding it out to the girl.

Persephone grinned. "Exactly." She grabbed a napkin and proceeded to draw a quick map of the Underworld. Then she showed it to Iris, pointing out the Elysian Fields. "It's the Underworld's most desirable neighborhood, and those lucky enough to go there get to feast, play, and sing forevermore."

After drawing more circles to indicate other areas of the Underworld, including asphodel fields, gloomy areas of swamp, and Tartarus, she pointed the tip of the pen toward a squiggly outline that encircled everything she'd drawn so far. "That's the River Styx, the boundary between Earth and the Underworld. Its source is a spring that plunges down a rocky cliff high above the river. It flows as a waterfall through a deep gorge and forms the river."

"What about the goddess that guards the river?"

"The Goddess Styx?" Persephone shrugged, causing her pretty red hair to shift back over one shoulder. "I've never met her, but I wave to her when I'm crossing her river on Charon's ferryboat. Her house is under the waterfall, and she watches that boat like a hawk. I think she's always hoping someone will fall out."

Just then the MOA herald appeared in the cafeteria and struck his lyrebell. "Attention, MOA students! First period begins in five minutes. Please continue to your classes without further ado."

Persephone gathered up her tray and textscrolls and stood to go. "Hope that helps," she said with a smile.

Iris nodded. "Definitely. Thanks!" A second later another question occurred to her, though, so she followed Persephone to the tray return. "Just one more thing. What would happen if someone did fall out of Charon's ferryboat?"

Persephone pretended to take a big bite of something

in a funny, dramatic way. "Chomp! They'd get eaten. Terrible things lurk in that ooky river."

"Oh," Iris said weakly. "Thanks." As she stood there digesting that information, she noticed Antheia looking around for her. Quickly she ducked behind the tray return, then sneaked out of the cafeteria. If Antheia caught her, she might ask her again to write that secret crush letterscroll to Zephyr. Or she might worm information out of Iris about her mission to the Underworld. A mission that could turn out to be dangerous. Yet, despite her fears she was determined to go get that pitcher from the goddess. And without Antheia. She wouldn't want to put her BFF in danger too!

Iris slipped down the hall to the front office. If she was going to see the Goddess Styx this morning, she would have to get permission to cut her first three classes. Fingers crossed, she went up to Ms. Hydra's tall desk and lurked at the end of a long line of students till she caught the blue head's attention.

"Oh, hi, Ms. Hydra," Iris said, speaking casually to the blue head when she saw her chance. "Zeus gave me an assignment to go to the Underworld but forgot to give me an Underworld pass."

That was like a hall pass, only it allowed a student to miss class time to go to the Underworld. You could also get an Earth pass and other kinds of passes if you had a good reason for one and were lucky enough to get to talk to Ms. Hydra's blue head. You could usually convince it to do whatever you wanted—as long as it was a halfway reasonable request.

"Certainly, dear," said the blue head. Luckily, Ms. Hydra's nosy, gossipy pink head was busy with another student right then, or it would probably have demanded to know exactly what she'd be doing in the Underworld.

As soon as Iris held the pass in her hand, she thanked the blue head and dashed off.

Chink! Chink!

On the way out of school, she heard chopping sounds. Zephyr and his three brothers were posing for the new anemometer in the courtyard. Meanwhile, the famous sculptor Pygmalion was busily whacking a hammer in order to chisel off a big piece of marble. At least Pheme had gotten it right about the sculptor's part in things.

The four brothers were flexing their muscles and grinning broadly toward the sculptor, apparently hoping to be depicted in marble for all eternity in what they considered to be distinguished, manly stances. Each was elbowing the other for the most prominent spot—front and center—on the anemometer. It would be cool to have the device at the Academy. Iris only hoped she made it back from the Underworld in one piece so that she would get to see it in action.

As she sat on the front steps to put on her winged sandals, she heard Zephyr say to Pygmalion, "I should be in front. I'm the most popular wind, after all. Warm, calm, springtimey."

Huh? He sounded as boastful as Boreas!

Boreas countered, saying, "No way! I've got that spot, Bro. Mine are the first winds of the year in January, so I should be first up on the statue. Besides that, I'm the wind that makes mortals cower. Cold and strong. That's me!"

"So? What about me?" said Eurus. "The east wind of autumn can get almost as cold as you, Boreas. And when people least expect it."

"Yeah, but my hot south winds can get pretty brutal in summer too," Notus put in. "Ask anyone."

"You guys only *wish* you were as important as me," Boreas told them, giving Notus and Eurus both noogies.

"Hey! Ow!" the two brothers protested.

While the laces on Iris's sandals were twining around her ankles, the four winds went on arguing, one-upping each other with reasons why they should get the prime spot in the sculpture. It surprised Iris that Zephyr was acting as arrogant as Boreas. Which was the *real* Zephyr? This one? Or the one she'd fallen in like with in her sisters' cafe?

Remembering something she wanted to ask him, she skimmed over to the boys.

"Well, if it isn't the Susie Sunshine Happy Harpy Rainbow Girl," called Boreas when he caught sight of her. Then he cracked up.

"Ha-ha," she murmured. She turned to Zephyr. "Got a minute?"

He arched a brow at her. "I'm kind of busy."

Like the boasts she'd just heard him make, his haughty tone surprised her. And it kind of hurt her feelings too. Still, there was something she wanted to know, so she pulled him aside. "Zeus is gone," she told him. "And I'm wondering why he would leave Mount Olympus when there could be a Typhon crisis any minute."

Zephyr looked uncertain. "I'm not really supposed to be talking about this with any MOA students."

Iris stepped closer so as not to be overheard. "Is it all part of a master plan to save the Academy?" she said, growing excited. "Did Zeus leave to draw T. away?" She studied the look of astonishment on Zephyr's face and was sure she had her answer. "Aha! I'm right."

"Zeph and Harpy sittin' in a tree. *K-I-S-S-I-N-G*," Boreas called to them, his voice teasing. Then he cracked up again. His brothers laughed too, though not as hard.

It was like they all considered Boreas the boss and let him get away with whatever he wanted. Despite the fact that he was a bully!

It really hurt that not even Zephyr stood up for her against his brother's teasing. Maybe she was better off letting Antheia have him after all! she thought in annoyance.

"Okay. Well . . ." She started backing away.

"Wait!" Zephyr took a step toward her, looking kind of sorry now, but she turned her back on him.

"See you," she called over her shoulder.

Her winged sandals helped her make a quick escape. However, instead of taking off for the Underworld right away, she zipped up MOA's front steps. Returning to the first floor of the Academy, she whirred through the halls. Wearing winged sandals inside the school was against the rules. She hoped no one saw. But she was fueled by the need to cut off any chance she'd thought she might have with Zephyr. Right now! So there could be no going back.

Opening her bag, Iris grabbed the blank letterscroll Antheia had given her and sat on a bench against a wall. Then she whipped out her pens and smoothed out the scroll on her lap. As she began crafting the secret crush notescroll Antheia had requested, she was still steaming mad at the boy. But as she considered what to say, she was reminded of the nice Zephyr she'd talked with at the café. And this is what she wrote:

I LIKE THE WAY YOU FLIP YOUR HAIR.

I LIKE YOUR GRAY-BLUE TWINKLY STARE.

I LIKE THE WAY YOU WHOOSH THE AIR.

I THINK WE'D MAKE AN AWESOME PAIR!

SIGNED,

YOUR SECRET CRUSH

Once she was finished, she rolled up the notescroll and tied it with a ribbon. It wasn't necessarily her best writing ever. Not bad for spur of the moment, though. She didn't add a name on the outside of the scroll. Antheia would know who it was for.

Her sandals whooshed her over to first-period Hero-ology class. Peeking around the edge of the open door, she saw that Mr. Cyclops was writing on the board. His back was to her. Medusa was seated in the row closest to the door. When the snake-haired girl happened to look over, Iris held up the notescroll and silently mouthed Antheia's name, also pointing toward where she was sitting across the room.

Nodding to show that she'd understood, Medusa quietly left her seat in the class. After sneaking over and taking the notescroll, she quickly folded it small and slipped it into the pocket of her chiton. Unfortunately,

Mr. Cyclops turned around and spotted her in the doorway just then. Iris ducked out of sight in the nick of time. Acting cool, Medusa casually shut the door as if closing it had been the reason she'd come over to begin with.

Iris stood out in the hall and watched through the vertical pane of glass in the door as Medusa sat down. The snake-haired girl immediately whispered something to the violet-eyed Dionysus, then slipped the notescroll from her pocket and passed it to him. Being careful to make sure Mr. Cyclops wouldn't notice, Dionysus passed the notescroll to Eros, who passed it to another student, and so on across the classroom.

In a matter of seconds it was in Antheia's possession. She ducked down so the teacher wouldn't see and opened it. When she realized it was the crush notescroll she'd requested, she glanced around until she spied Iris through the glass pane. Smiling gratefully, Antheia gave her a thumbs-up. Iris waved and grinned back. Then she headed off before the teacher could see her, her good deed done.

Feeling pleased with herself, she let her winged sandals carry her to the front doors of the Academy. She might not have followed through with writing that crush note if Zephyr hadn't acted the way he had out in the courtyard, so maybe it was a good thing he had! By writing the note for Antheia, she hoped she'd put any feelings she had for that boy behind her once and for all.

She pushed out through the front doors. Then she was off, speeding past the four windy boys on her way to the Underworld. She didn't even look their way!

As Iris took to the air, she practiced her rainbows, trying to take her mind off the scary nature of what she was about to do. Each rainbow she made arced farther than the previous one and with better aim. She was improving for sure. Maybe by the time she got back to the Academy, her skills would be honed enough to prove her worthiness as goddessgirl of rainbows. Delivering the pitcher to Zeus would put him in a good mood, so the timing would be perfect!

Now and then as she traveled, she checked Persephone's map to make sure she was going the right way. All too soon she landed on the riverbank. Just like Persephone had described, there was a waterfall that plunged down a rocky cliff high above her and into a deep gorge, where it became the dismal, murky River Styx that rushed past the bank where she stood. This had to be the place. But where was the Goddess Styx's house?

Squinting at the side of the cliff for a while, Iris finally spotted something under the waterfall. A room-size ledge. A table and other furniture sat on it, and dug into the side of the cliff behind it were shelves and a hearth. It was all completely open to the outside.

She gazed down into the ooky muddy gray water below, more than a little worried. It was a long way up to that cliff house, higher than she was used to flying in her sandals. Should she try traveling by rainbow? Could she make one sturdy enough to hold her weight? If it wobbled and failed her, she'd fall, and something lurking in this water might do her in. Crocodiles. Or some kind of wild, watery beast. She shuddered at the thought.

No, she didn't feel quite brave enough to chance it with a rainbow. Not yet. Still, she hadn't come all this way just to give up. Before she could change her mind, she leaned forward and let her winged sandals whoosh her upward and across the gorge. She ducked under the waterfall to land on the high ledge on the far side. There, she wrapped the laces of her sandals around the silver wings to keep them still so she could walk normally.

There was a fire burning in the hearth, but Iris didn't see anyone around. She called out anyway just to be sure. "Hello? Goddess Styx?"

There was no answer, so she looked around, hoping to spot the pitcher herself. In every nook and cranny of the cliff wall, there were keepsakes. Three tiny blue salamander eggs had been tucked into one nook. A bundle of birch twigs tied with string had been tucked into another. A jar of iridescent fish scales sat on a shelf, along with other oddball items she didn't wish to examine too carefully.

The mantel above the hearth was stacked full of framed *Greekly Weekly News* clippings. Many were stories about the Olympic Games that were held at MOA every four years. Squinting, Iris stared at some of the pictures—Otus and Ephialtes. Two Titan boys! She remembered they'd come to the Academy for the Boys' Olympics a while back and had caused a ton of trouble. But then she noticed some pro-Olympian stuff too. A drawing of Apollo receiving a target-shooting award, and Ares getting a javelin-throwing one.

Iris's mind boggled. There was a long history of distrust between Olympian gods and the Titans, dating back to that long-ago war between them that Zephyr had mentioned. So who had the Goddess actually favored? Not sure she wanted to find out, Iris started to back away.

As she turned to go, there, sitting right on a table made out of a tree stump was . . . a pitcher! She'd been so busy checking out the items in the nooks and crannies in the cliff wall that she'd missed seeing the very object she's come here for. It was teal colored with a stopper in the top. Since there were no other pitchers around, this surely had to be the one Zeus desired.

Growing excited, Iris whipped out her pens. She was about to write a quick note to the goddess explaining that she'd borrowed the pitcher for Zeus and would return it later, when she thought to look inside it.

Oh no! It was empty. Zeus had said it would contain water. What now? Before she could decide what to do, she heard splashing. She glanced down from the ledge in time to see a whirling dervish spin up and out of the river below. It headed right for her!

In mere seconds it reached the ledge where Iris stood. A gray face with piercing eyes peered out at her from the middle of the dervish as it whirled around and around, dripping water onto her. Startled, Iris stumbled backward against the cliff wall. Was this the Goddess Styx?

8
Pitcher Snatcher

"PITCHER SNATCHER!" THE DERVISH ACCUSED when she saw what Iris held. "Nobody steals from the Goddess Styx! Well, what have ye to say for yourself, thief?" She darted close, and Iris jumped away from her. *Eek!* In her attempt to escape, she'd almost stepped into the fire!

"I'm not a pitcher snatcher. I mean, I wasn't stealing it. I was going to leave a note," Iris sputtered. She clutched the pitcher and her bag to her chest, wishing with all her heart that she hadn't ventured here after all. What had she gotten herself into?

"A likely story! Who are ye and what are ye up to?" demanded Styx, still spinning round and round. What if this goddess decided to toss her into the river below? Or worse yet, into Tartarus? Even immortals could wind up there if they offended more powerful gods and goddesses. Judging by the expression of outrage on Styx's face, Iris had definitely offended her!

Still clinging to the wall behind her, Iris took a few quick breaths. She needed to be brave, and the bravest goddessgirl she knew was Artemis. *So, what would Artemis do in this situation?* she wondered. The answer came into her head immediately. Stand up for herself, that's what!

"I'm Iris, the Goddess of Rainbows," she announced,

straightening. The fib about her being in charge of rainbows slipped out without her intending it to. But she had a feeling Styx wouldn't let her take the pitcher if she admitted the truth. That although she *was* an MOA student and an immortal, she *wasn't* important enough to be the goddess of anything in particular. "And like I said, I just want to borrow your pitcher. I promise to bring it back. So I'll just be going . . ." She started sidling away.

The spinning, drippy goddess swooped down and skidded to a stop on the ledge, instantly taking the shape of a woman. A woman made of swirling, swampy, sludgy water with long strands of water-hair floating wildly around her face.

"Not so fast," she said. She lunged toward Iris, who scrambled away from her. Unfortunately, in her hurry to get away from the river goddess, she came too close to the cliff's edge. As the goddess caught up to her and yanked the pitcher from her hands, Iris fell right off the ledge!

Nooo! Down, down, down she plummeted. The wind rushed by her ears as she somersaulted head over heels into the gorge. Unable to keep hold of her bag, she dropped it, then watched it plunge into the thick, icky, sludge-gray waves of the river below, lost forever. So much for Ceyx's letterscroll to Hera. No time to worry about that now. She had to save herself from the same fate.

No time to release her sandals' wings. She'd have to take a chance. . . .

Brrrng! The familiar sound like the strum of a harp filled the gorge as Iris desperately hurled a ball of magic to the far side of the riverbank below. As color streamed from her fingers, a rainbow arced a dozen feet below her, stretching from the gorge wall down to the opposite bank of the River Styx.

Thump! Iris landed on the rainbow. It was slippery, and she fell halfway off it at once, but somehow she managed to hold on to its edge, gain a foothold, and then swing herself atop the shimmery rainbow.

"What's going on up there-ere-ere?" shouted a new voice. It was very deep and it echoed, as if it came from deep within a cave.

Heart pounding after her near disaster, Iris kneeled on the rainbow and searched high and low for the source of the voice. Seeing no one, she glanced down toward the safety that waited at the bottom end of the rainbow on the riverbank. She wanted nothing more than to head home to MOA and forget all about this disastrous mission. Turning her head to look the other way, she saw that Styx was just staring at her from the craggy ledge with the pitcher clutched in her hands. Probably hoping Iris would land in the river and get eaten by whoever or whatever had just spoken!

Humph, thought Iris, feeling indignant. "We'll see about that!" Then before she could change her mind, she gathered every single scrap of courage she possessed and slid up the rainbow to land on the ledge beside Styx again. "I'm back!" she announced.

But instead of acting annoyed, Styx was all twitchy now, looking around as if expecting a boogeyman to jump out at them at any moment.

"What's going on-on-on?" It was that voice again.

A crack formed in the ledge by Iris's feet. *Eek!* She jumped away as the crack widened. The earth split open, and another woman sprang out from it, this one sculpted from mud and rock. She stared Iris in the eye.

Before the rock woman could speak, the Goddess Styx gave her a fake, sarcastic smile. "Gaia! How nice of you to drop by. I haven't seen you since—"

"The war," Gaia finished for her, but her attention was on Iris. "So you have a visitor?" she said to Styx. "An Olympian by the stench of her, and by the loook of her glittery skinny skin skin."

This was Gaia? The Earth goddess? thought Iris. Well, if anyone stank around here, it was Gaia, not her. The goddess smelled like rotting leaves, wormy tree trunks, toadstools, and dank soil. Up close Iris could see that cobwebs, small bones, and bits of moss were tangled in the goddess's mud-covered hair. *Eew!*

More than ever, Iris wanted out of there. But she needed that pitcher! If she could've seen her own aura right now, she knew it would be more chicken yellow (which was a totally different shade from happy, sunny yellow) than courageous red. Because she was shaking in her sandals.

Gaia walked around her. Iris twisted her head as the

Earth goddess circled her. "Olympians are so annoying," the goddess muttered.

"And Titans aren't?" scoffed Styx.

"You dare insult my son?" huffed Gaia.

"Typhon's an idiot. A doofus."

At that, Iris's ears perked up, and her eyes widened in alarm. *Typhon was Gaia's son?*

"And you think Olympians are sooo smart?" Gaia countered. Her gaze narrowed on Iris. "Let's test this one then," she said.

"And just why have you come here, Miss Smartypants?" she asked Iris.

Smart? That made Iris think of Athena. If faced with such a question, that brainy goddessgirl would probably answer it directly, but also in a way that made clear what she wanted. That would be the smart thing to do.

"I want the pitcher. And I want it filled with water this time," Iris replied in a firm tone.

"Well, where's your hospitality? Fill your pitcher for the girl," Gaia told Styx. "She's obviously thirsty." A look passed between the two goddesses that Iris couldn't decipher.

"Okay, bossy-pants," Styx replied to Gaia. Taking the pitcher, she leaped off the ledge. *Splash!* Into the river she went.

While she was gone, Gaia glanced at Iris, then turned her attention to the mantel and the news clippings upon it. "I too once championed the Olympians, did you know that, little girl? But no more." One by one she carelessly knocked the framed Olympian news clippings into the fire. Then she straightened the remaining Titan ones, smiling fondly at one in particular.

Craning her neck, Iris read the title: ANOTHER TITAN

VICTORY. A closer look enabled her to read a name: *T-Y-P-H-O-N.* Typhon? Gaia's son—the monster determined to destroy Zeus—must be a Titan! Which made total sense. Typhon probably had a grudge against Zeus because he'd locked up the beast after the war.

Gaia seemed to forget that Iris was there for a moment, for she murmured, "Ah, my dear son. You'll make Mama proud soon, won't you?"

Suddenly Iris put two and two together. Zeus had said someone had released Typhon from Tartarus. It must have been Gaia! Iris needed to get out of here, fast, and let Zeus know!

As if sensing her thoughts, the goddess shot her a look. "If you really want to take that pitcher with you, you'll have to drink from it first to pass a test. One in which there are consequences for failure."

Just then, Styx reappeared, having obviously

overheard. "Drink up," she said, handing the pitcher to Iris.

Before she held it to her mouth, Iris peered closely at the pitcher, noticing for the first time the words engraved on it. They blended into an etched pattern, making them difficult to see at first glance. The words were:

Anyone who drinks and lies
Is in for a very unpleasant surprise.

Iris didn't like the sound of that. Was the pitcher some kind of lie detector? How did Zeus think that would help save the school from Typhon?

"What's the unpleasant surprise?" she asked, looking between the goddesses.

Gaia let out an evil cackle. "That's for us to know and you to avoid finding out. Now drink from the pitcher.

Then I'll ask you three questions. If you answer truthfully, all will be well."

And what if I don't? Iris wondered. She shook her head. "Eew! I'm sorry, but that river water looked too icky to drink."

Rolling her eyes, Styx took the pitcher and dribbled water from it onto the floor. Somehow it had become sparkling and pure! Still a bit wary, Iris reclaimed the pitcher, tipped it toward her mouth, and took a swallow of the cold water. It tasted wonderful!

"It's my pitcher. I'll ask the first question," said Styx.

But Gaia, who had stepped closer and begun to circle Iris where she stood, beat the river goddess to the punch. "Are you really from the Academy?" she asked.

"Yes," Iris answered easily, turning her head to keep track of the goddess. "So this pitcher is some kind of lie detector, right?"

Gaia frowned. "Don't answer a question with a question if you truly want the pitcher. Now where is Zeus? Rumor has it he's not on Mount Olympus."

"I don't know his exact location right now," Iris replied quickly. Which was true. She believed him to be at the Gray Ladies' office. But since she'd never been there herself, she had no idea where that was exactly.

"The next question is mine," said Styx.

"Hush, fool," snarked Gaia.

"You hush. It's my pitcher. I'll ask the next question," argued Styx.

"Just try it," challenged Gaia.

And just like that, the goddesses began to fight. They twirled and twisted around and around each other. Water mixed with earth, and before long they turned into a great big ball of angry, writhing sludge. Talk about eew!

Iris slipped on the sludge as it oozed across the ledge

toward her. Yelping, she barely managed to hang on to the pitcher as she found herself falling toward doom once again. Her last rainbow had faded by now. She had no choice but to try her luck again with another one. And this time she was going to need to make a really, really long, *huge* rainbow—one that would whisk her all the way to MOA! With all her might she threw out a new ball of magic. *Brrrng!*

"Ow! Hey! Not bad!" she murmured encouragingly to herself when she landed upon the new rainbow she'd caused to appear. Indeed, it *looked* and felt pretty sturdy. And it stretched so far into the distance that she couldn't see where it ended.

She could still hear the goddesses raging at each other in the gorge behind her. How much time before they noticed she was gone?

Feeling kind of brave after her success in getting the

pitcher, she zipped up the bands of colored light and sailed away from the River Styx.

However, when she reached the very top of the arc—about halfway to MOA—her rainbow suddenly gave a hard wobble. Oh no! And then she was falling—for the third time that day! She'd failed at making a travel-worthy rainbow after all. Would those two angry goddesses be waiting for her at the bottom, having finally realized she'd stolen the pitcher while they'd been fighting?

All at once, strong hands grabbed her arm in midair and pulled her upward. She clung to the pitcher with her free hand, refusing to let it fall. Seconds later she was lifted onto a cushion of wind. As she righted herself, she pushed her hair out of her face and found herself staring into a pair of worried blue eyes. Saved! By . . . Zephyr?

"You!" she yelped. Recovering from her surprise, she

quickly added a grateful "Thank-you!" Then she asked, "But where did you come from? How did you know where to find—"

"I didn't," he interrupted. "But I'm glad I found you. Trouble's brewing, and I was worried about you. Just look around!"

Iris did. The sky was noticeably darker than it had been even a few minutes before. In fact, the atmosphere all around them had turned a dusky, roiling gray. Maybe the brewing weather was the reason her rainbow had wobbled. The notion gave her hope that another try might prove she could in fact create a sturdy rainbow that would support her travels.

Suddenly realizing the true significance of the frighteningly wild winds around them, she blurted, "Oh no! Is this . . . Typhon's doing?"

Zephyr nodded. "Looks like he's on the way to

MOA at last. Come on. Let's get back there."

Tucking the pitcher under one arm, Iris reached to release the straps that bound the wings on her sandals. She wasn't ready to chance it with another rainbow yet, not after that last fall.

"No need for that," said Zephyr, stopping her. "My winds will whip us there in no time."

As the two of them were swept away on a swirling pillow of air, she felt him glance at her a few times. Then finally he said, "I'm sorry for not standing up for you in the courtyard today. For how I acted and all. I hope I didn't hurt your feelings."

"It's okay," Iris said, not really wanting to talk about it.

"No, it's not," he insisted. "My brothers and I are pretty competitive. But Boreas is always the one who gets noticed. I guess I was just showing off, trying to beat him at his own game for once. Of course, the anemometer is just a cover for the real reason we're at MOA. Still, I admit I really kind of wanted to be the one featured on it."

Iris nodded, softening toward him. "I get it. The frustration and wanting to stand out, I mean. I don't want to be like my sisters, but sometimes it's annoying that people always notice the trouble they get into but not the trouble I stay out of."

He nodded, seeming glad that she understood.

"Not only that," she went on, "it can be hard to stand out at MOA, too. I'm not brainy like Athena, or good at matchmaking like Aphrodite, or brave like Artemis, or good with flowers like Persephone, or wreaths like Antheia. In fact, I'm not the official goddess of anything."

"Huh? That's weird. I thought all goddesses were in charge of something. I assumed you were the goddess of rainbows. You're a natural at making them."

She gave him a pleased smile. "Think so?"

"Yeah, I do," Zephyr said earnestly. "And I should know, since I'm a bit of a weather specialist myself!"

"Thanks." Suddenly the cushion of air under them gave a series of lurches and began to feel less steady. She sent Zephyr a worried look.

"Typhon's winds are making the atmosphere unstable. But he's actually still a ways off by my estimation. I'll get us to MOA safely. Never fear," he assured her. To distract her he started forming animal shapes in the curls of wind as they traveled, which did lighten the mood a little. He made chickens that pecked, whipping them up out of thin air, sort of like cloud animals. Then he made horses that leaped, and lastly sheep like the ones that dotted the rolling green hills below them.

"Those aren't half *baaad*," Iris commented, mimicking the sound of a sheep. They both laughed. As their giggles died away, she couldn't help saying, "You don't ever need to be like your blowhard brothers, you know. Because you're already cool just the way you are. I mean, I know you're the *warm* wind. What I meant was just that . . . "

He flipped a lock of chestnut hair out of his eyes and looked over at her, a slow grin filling his face. "I know what you meant. And I think the same about you. Let's face it—we're both cool!" The two of them laughed.

And just like that, all the fluttery liking feelings she'd had for him earlier came flooding back. Plus, the way he was gazing at her right then made her feel as beautiful as Aphrodite!

She wondered if he'd found the secret crush letter-scroll that she'd written and that Antheia had probably put someplace where he'd be sure to find it easily.

Should she tell him what she'd done? Stop things before they got started? She bit her lower lip, tugging at it with her teeth. Then she opened her mouth, not sure what she was going to say.

"Looks like Zeus is finally back," Zephyr announced, looking downward as they approached the Academy. "He must've given up on trying to draw Typhon out for now."

"Oh!" said Iris, snapping out of her crush-induced haze. She looked down to see that Pegasus was landing in the courtyard below with Zeus. And Hera's peacock-drawn chariot was right behind.

By the time Iris and Zephyr reached the courtyard themselves, Zeus and Hera had already gone into the school. Iris said a quick farewell to Zephyr and then raced to Zeus's office, where she zoomed past Ms. Hydra without stopping. Without bothering to knock on the principal's door, she dashed inside and headed for his desk. Her view of it was blocked by the file cabinets in the middle of the room, but as she began to skirt around them, she heard voices. Zeus's and Hera's.

"So about that letterscroll you wrote to Ceyx," Zeus was saying.

"What? How did you know about that? Have you been snooping?" Hera demanded, sounding a little worried. And Iris knew why. Hera didn't want Zeus to find out about those pet names Ceyx and Alcyone were using and start pitching thunderbolts at them because he thought they were being disrespectful.

"Who, me? No!" Zeus replied to Hera. "But the Gray Ladies said I need better communication skills. So if there's some problem, I think you should communicate it to me and let me handle it, sugarplum. After all, I'm King of the Gods and Ruler of the Heavens."

"You think you're the only one who can handle a problem?" asked Hera, sounding a little annoyed now. "Well, you'll just have to trust that I can handle this one."

"Aha! So you admit there *is* a problem!" crowed Zeus. "Then—"

Iris was still moving full tilt when she slipped on something gooey on the floor. Sliding past the file cabinets, she then slammed into Zeus's desk and came to a halt. Zeus and Hera looked down at her in surprise.

"I've got it! I've got the pitcher!" she yelled. She held it out, and Zeus took it.

"Oh, good," Zeus said, his face lighting up. "Just what I need."

Before Iris could tell him where she'd found the pitcher and her concerns about it, he unstoppered it and turned to Hera.

"Hera, honeybun," he said, giving her a wide, fake-looking grin. "This is such an interesting discussion. Why don't we talk a bit more about it? But take a drink first before you go on. You look thirsty."

Zeus obviously already knew that the pitcher was a lie detector, Iris realized. And he was going to give the truth water to Hera to pump her for information about Ceyx and Alcyone! Who cared about those two birdbrains? Was this the only reason he'd had her fetch the pitcher?

"What about Typhon. I thought you needed the pitcher to fight him," she said, aghast.

"What?" Zeus's bushy red eyebrows slammed together. "What do you know about Typhon?" he demanded, somehow managing to look angry, confused, and concerned all at the same time.

"I overheard you talking about him in your office yesterday." Iris explained. Then in a flood of words she went on to tell him and Hera about her trip to the Underworld and about getting the pitcher from Styx and Gaia. But before she could question Zeus about its magical lie-detecting powers, he waved her off.

"Okay, okay. Run along now," he said quickly. "You did well, fetching this. We'll talk more later."

"But isn't that thing dangerous—" Iris tried again.

"No! Shoo!" he boomed.

Iris shooed. As she left, she heard Hera ask him, "What was that all about?"

"Nothing to worry over," said Zeus. "Now about that other matter . . ."

If that was Zeus's idea of communication, he had work to do! thought Iris. Once outside the office, she walked down the hallway, totally flummoxed. What was going on? Zeus didn't seem worried about the pitcher, but his mind seemed to be so focused on Hera right now that he wasn't paying proper attention to the threat from Typhon. Was it possible Zeus hadn't even told Hera about Typhon? Did he think her such a delicate flower that she couldn't handle the news? That seemed like a big mistake to Iris. Grown-ups! Sometimes they were completely baffling.

Third period was over by now and everyone was at lunch. After grabbing a quick snack from the snacks table in the cafeteria, Iris went by her dorm room, found a new bag to replace the one she'd lost in the river, and stuffed an assortment of colorful pens and some lip gloss inside it. Once downstairs again, she took off her winged sandals. Remembering that she'd left her own sandals on the steps, she went outside to retrieve them. The sky didn't look any worse, so Typhon wasn't making his move yet.

Just then she realized she'd forgotten to tell Hera

that she'd lost Ceyx's reply scroll. Nor had she told her that Ceyx had promised not to use the pet names anymore. Should she go back to the office and—

"Psst!" Someone was trying to get her attention. Iris looked around. She spotted Antheia calling to her from the olive grove across the courtyard. Wondering what was up, she headed toward it. The grove of silvery-green olive trees had been Athena's creation, built shortly after that brainy goddessgirl's invention of the olive had won her the right to have the city of Athens named after her.

The moment Iris entered the grove, Antheia drew her to a place thick with trees where they'd be sheltered from prying eyes. Then the girl started jumping up and down with glee. "Zephyr got our secret crush letter-scroll!" she squealed in delight.

Iris's stomach clenched. *Oh, goody,* she thought. *Not!*

9

Secret Crush

HOW DO YOU KNOW HE GOT THE SECRET CRUSH scroll?" asked Iris, hoping Antheia might be mistaken.

"I flattened it and poked it through the vent slits in his locker door, and a few minutes ago when I was in the hall, I saw him pull it out." Antheia's eyes were twinkling. "And guess what? He grinned when he read it! Like he'd guessed who it was from and was glad it was me. Squeee!"

She hopped around in a little circle, as happy as could

be. Her aura showed she was tickled pink. The opposite of how Iris was feeling. "But you haven't even talked to him, so how can you be sure Zephyr knows the note was from you?"

"I *did* talk to him, though," Antheia informed her. "In the hall this morning after first period."

"Oh." Iris's heart sank. "What did you say?" she couldn't help asking.

Antheia shrugged. "Just small talk. You know, like I asked him about the sculpture."

"And what did he tell you?" Even though it hurt to keep talking about this, Iris felt like she *had* to find out if Antheia was right about Zephyr's feelings.

"He told me all about it. I kind of zoned out when he explained about the cups catching the wind or whatever. But then he asked me how long you and I have been BFFs and how we met and stuff," Antheia replied. "That's the kind of information a boy asks when he wants to get to know a girl he likes, don't you think?"

Iris nodded wistfully. "I guess so," she said. But she didn't really know. She'd never gotten very far with either of her two previous crushes. Both crushes had been nipped in the bud by Antheia—just like *this* crush! Iris leaned back against the strong trunk of an olive tree, causing some of its silvery-green leaves to flutter to the ground.

"So . . . will you?" Antheia asked a minute or so later.

Iris stood straighter, wondering what she'd missed. "Will I what?"

"Write another crush letter to him for me?"

"So soon after the first one?" Iris asked, her throat tightening.

"I don't want to miss my chance. He and his brothers could be gone from here any day now. I want you to ask him to meet me in the olive grove if he's interested in hanging out with me."

Iris bit down on her bottom lip. She really didn't want to be involved in this anymore, but she didn't know how to get out of it. "Sorry, I don't have a blank letterscroll, so—" she started to say.

"Ta-da!" Antheia said in a triumphant voice, whipping one out of her bag. "Be prepared. That's my motto—don't wear it out."

Reluctantly Iris got out her pens. She should never have written that first letter, but since she had, it seemed she was duty-bound to write a second. "My new motto is never write another secret crush note," she muttered under her breath.

"You don't really mind, do you?" Antheia asked anxiously.

Iris's heart ached to see the hope and excitement in her

friend's eyes. "No, not a bit," she said, forcing a smile. She wouldn't disappoint Antheia. "Let's see . . ." She stared off into space and quickly made up a riddle on the fly:

WHAT'S THE OPPOSITE OF WON'T?

____

WHAT LETTER COMES AFTER T?

____

WHAT'S THE OPPOSITE OF STOP?

____

WHAT'S THE OPPOSITE OF IN? ________

"LONG" IS TO "LENGTH" AS "WIDE" IS TO

____

DO RE ___ FA SO LA TI DO!

IF THE ANSWER IS YES, MEET ME IN THE OLIVE GROVE AFTER SCHOOL AT 3:30 TODAY.

SIGNED,

YOUR SECRET CRUSH

"Will. U. Go. Out. Width. Me. It's brilliant!" crowed Antheia. She took the scroll and started rolling it up. "Since he and his brothers are posing for their sculpture again in the courtyard, now's the perfect time to deliver it to his locker. Only, I have to get to fourth period early today, and it's the other direction from his locker. Think you could do it for me? And could you maybe add some colorful decorations to the note before you do?"

"Wait. That's not—" Iris began to protest. But before she could finish saying "part of the deal," Antheia handed the scroll back to her and told her Zephyr's locker number.

"Thanks, Iris. You're the best!" Antheia gave her a big hug, then dashed off.

"Ye gods! They're coming this way! I don't want them to think we're spying. Let's hide in here," she heard Athena say a minute later. Iris looked up from the bench inside the grove, where she'd sat to decorate the secret crush letterscroll, as Antheia had requested. A second later Athena, Aphrodite, and Artemis zoomed into the grove, looking rather frantic. They spotted Iris right away and waved to her to take cover with them behind a nearby clump of olive trees.

As Iris joined them, Aphrodite peered toward the entrance to the grove. "Oh no! They're heading in here too," she moaned.

"Who are we hiding from?" Iris whispered. But then she heard a voice and she knew.

"Are you sure you aren't thirsty, sweetie pie?" It was Principal Zeus. Iris peeked out from between two branches and saw that he'd entered the grove with Hera. And he was holding Styx's pitcher out to her. He was still trying to get her to drink from it!

"Not really," Hera replied, shaking her head.

"Have some of these ambrosia chips I brought along. They'll help you work up a thirst."

"No, thanks."

Zeus's attempt to get Hera to drink from the pitcher was so comical that Iris had to stifle a giggle. Like the other girls, she didn't want to be discovered eavesdropping on the King of the Gods.

"I know!" said Zeus. "We should go for a jog. The exercise would do us good. Ten miles or so ought to do it. I'll just bring this pitcher of water in case you get thirsty along the way."

Hera eyed the pitcher, obviously suspicious of how hard he was trying to get her to drink from it.

"Why is he so dead set on getting her to drink from that pitcher?" Artemis whispered.

Aphrodite shrugged. "You got me."

"Remember what Pheme said about my dad and Hera seeking counseling? It's true," Athena informed them. "They went to see the Gray Ladies."

"The school counselors?" Aphrodite whispered in surprise. "What's that got to do with the pitcher?"

Athena shook her head. "No clue. But I wish I knew why they went to see those counselors. It's got me kind of worried—"

"In the cafeteria, I heard Pheme say it had something to do with bad vacations," said Artemis.

"No, it's—" Iris tried to say.

"I thought she said it was some problem with education," Aphrodite said at the same time. "But I still don't get what that has to do with a pitcher."

"No!" As all eyes went to Iris, pent up words finally burst from her. "The pitcher's a lie detector, filled with truth water. I got it from the Goddess Styx." Watching Zeus and Hera, who were now too far across the grove to hear, she explained what she'd learned from visiting Ceyx and Alcyone, leaving out other details of her meeting in Zeus's office, since he'd asked her to keep mum.

"This whole problem is all about some dumb pet names?" Artemis rolled her eyes.

"It was just a comedy of errors," said Aphrodite, sounding relieved. "All we need to do is convince Principal Zeus of that."

"Hello? Have you met my dad?" Athena said. "That's not the sort of thing he'll take lightly. He has a bit of a temper, you know. And once he makes up his mind . . ."

They turned to see Zeus follow Hera toward the olive grove entrance. Suddenly she spun around and heaved a big sigh. It looked like she'd had enough of his badgering. She reached for the pitcher and lifted it to her lips.

"No!" Iris called out, unable to stop herself. She burst from the trees, with the other girls close behind her.

Zeus and Hera whipped around to stare at the girls in surprise.

"Ibis? Theeny?" Zeus said, getting Iris's name wrong again and calling Athena by his nickname for her. He didn't call the other goddessgirls by name at all. Possibly because he didn't remember their names? "What are you—"

"Are you sure that drinking from that pitcher isn't dangerous?" Iris asked Zeus. "Gaia and Styx thought so. See the inscription?" she said, pointing out the words on the pitcher. "It's hard to read because of the decoration, but . . ."

Squinting at it, Zeus read aloud:

"Anyone who drinks and lies

Is in for a very unpleasant surprise."

As understanding dawned, Zeus paled at what had almost happened. "'Unpleasant surprise'?" He glanced at Iris. "Is that what you meant in my office when you said it was dangerous?"

Iris nodded.

Hera gasped. "You mean that thing is a lie detector? With a kick? And you wanted to use it on me?"

Zeus nodded, looking more than a little chagrined. "I didn't know about the inscription, though. Really, I didn't! I'd never take a chance of anything unpleasant happening to you. Can you ever forgive me, sugar pie?"

Hera stared at him, one skeptical eyebrow raised.

Iris was pleased to see that Zeus looked pale at what could have happened, and repentant. He stared down at his feet. "You wrote a letterscroll to Ceyx," he mumbled. "And I heard a rumor that he was your secret admirer."

Pheme! thought Iris. She must have found out about the pet names somehow and spilled the birdseed, um, beans.

Hera folded her arms and tapped the toes of one sandaled foot, still looking annoyed. "That's what this was all about? Two lovebirds in the IM calling each other 'Zeus' and 'Hera'?" Then she quickly explained about the misunderstanding, including the part about the pet names.

"Sorry, my love," Zeus said sheepishly. "Still, you might have told me right away what was going on, and let me handle it. Good communication is a two-way street, you know, honeybun."

He had a point, thought Iris.

"You're right. I guess I should have told you. I was only trying to spare Ceyx and his wife from your anger," Hera said, sounding less annoyed now. "I was worried your temper would lead you to do something . . . regrettable."

Zeus grinned. "Something involving thunderbolts and smiting, you mean?" Then he turned more serious. "I'm sorry I lost my temper and flew off the handle. Honestly, I didn't have Iris fetch the pitcher to use it on you. I wanted it for . . ." He looked around the group and broke off what he'd been going to say.

"You're right that I would have gotten angry," Zeus conceded. "But you would have calmed me down in the end and kept me from doing anything too awful."

Like smiting a certain pair of birdbrain shopkeepers, thought Iris.

Zeus and Hera were looking at each other with lovey-dovey eyes now. Quickly Athena signaled to the other girls, and they all tiptoed out of the grove and made their way back to the Academy. They had just entered the main hall when the lyrebell rang for fourth period. Waving a quick good-bye, Iris hurried off.

The halls were pretty much empty by the time she found Zephyr's locker. After making sure the coast was clear, she pressed the crush letterscroll she'd written on behalf of Antheia against the lockers. Quickly she flattened it with the side of her fist, which allowed her to push it through one of the vent slots on the front of Zephyr's locker. Done!

Noticing the increasingly dark skies as she glanced out a window on her way to class afterward, she worried anew about Typhon. When would the Titan monster attack? Would Zeus and the wind-brothers be able to defeat him?

Just then she saw Zeus heading off on Pegasus. Alone. Where was he going? Not to the IM to smite Ceyx after all, she hoped. But shouldn't he be staying here to defend the Academy at a time like this?

. . .

After school was finally out for the day, Iris was about to head up to the dorms when Antheia ran over, looking freaked out. "In ten minutes it'll be three thirty!" she announced.

"You'd better get to the grove, then. If Zephyr's coming to meet you there, you don't want to be late," said Iris. She started to turn away because she really did not want to think about the crush that might soon blossom between those two.

Antheia shook her head, looking pale. There was a chicken-yellow halo around her whole body. "No! I can't do it. Not by myself. What if I don't know what to say to him? Can't you come to the olive grove and just stand nearby and whisper stuff for me to tell him?"

"What? That'll never work," said Iris, shaking her head emphatically.

"Just try it. Please, please, puh-*leeze*," begged Antheia. "I'm afraid that if I try to talk to him without your help, he'll guess that it wasn't me who wrote those secret crush letters. C'mon. I'm begging you."

Iris had never seen Antheia so panicked. "Okay . . . I'll come," she agreed hesitantly. *What have I gotten myself into?* she thought as she followed Antheia outside. She really did not want to be involved in this. Not. At. All.

The two girls hurried over to the olive grove. "Good. He's not here yet," Antheia noted, glancing around. She sat on the bench, which was positioned in front of an olive tree that grew thick with blue-green leaves. "Get behind the tree," she instructed.

"Huh?" Iris said.

"We can't let him see you. That would give it away. If

you hide behind me, you can whisper answers to whatever he says to me and I can repeat them to him, okay?"

Reluctantly Iris went behind the bench and hunkered down behind the tree.

"You okay back there?" Antheia asked after a few minutes had passed.

"Yes," Iris whispered back. "But I think this is a really bad idea. Think how embarrassing it'll be if—"

"Shh! Someone's coming," hissed Antheia. Then her voice changed to a sweet, flirty one, and she said, "Hi, Zephyr."

"Antheia? Where's Iris?" He sounded surprised and not altogether pleased, Iris decided. *Uh-oh.*

"Iris? Oh, I don't know where she is," Antheia fibbed. From her place in the bushes, Iris could see Antheia cross her fingers behind her back so as not to get jinxed by her own fib.

"But I thought . . . So the notescrolls were from you?" asked Zephyr.

Iris peeked out and saw him stick his hands into the pockets of his tunic. He shifted from one foot to the other, looking uncomfortable.

"Yes. Um . . ." A small silence fell.

Iris could tell that Antheia didn't know what to say next. The girl reached back, waving a hand behind her that only Iris could see. She wanted help.

Quickly Iris whispered. "Say this: 'So I'm glad you figured out the clues in my notescroll.'" Maybe that would get the conversation rolling.

"So, I'm glad you figured out the shoes in my notescroll," Antheia repeated brightly. Then she cleared her throat and said. "I mean the *clues* in my notescroll."

"Yeah, it was clever," he said. Silence again.

"Ask him how the anemometer is coming," whispered Iris. *Ye gods.* Was she going to have to carry the burden of this whole conversation?

"Ask him how . . . I mean, how is the anemometer coming?" said Antheia.

Iris groaned silently at Antheia's second bumble.

"Okay, I guess," Zephyr replied.

Antheia didn't seem to have a follow-up question, so Iris went on feeding her ideas. "Do you know when Pygmalion will finish it and if—"

"Did you just hear someone whispering?" Zephyr asked, looking around. He peered beyond the bench at the tree, his eyes searching among its branches. Iris froze, then curled into a ball, hiding as best she could.

"Whispering? No!" said Antheia, scooting over on the bench in the hopes of shielding Iris. But she sounded kind of guilty.

"I did," Zephyr insisted. "It was coming from somewhere behind you."

Before Iris could even try to get away, he ran around the tree. He looked as shocked to see her as she was to see him. Caught, she stood up.

"Iris? What are you doing here? Is this some kind of a joke?" He looked back and forth between the two girls.

"Yeah, we were just joking around," said Antheia, grinning weakly.

Zephyr stiffened, looking hurt. "Well, your little prank was not funny. Not at all." With that, he turned on his heel and stalked out of the olive grove.

"Huh? What went wrong?" Antheia said, staring after him with a look of surprise.

"He's mad and hurt!" exclaimed Iris. "He thinks we were playing a joke on him. Don't you get it? Imagine how you'd feel in *his* place."

"Oh no! This is a disaster. He'll never like me now!" Antheia leaped from the bench and rushed off in tears.

Iris ran out of the grove after her, then paused. Zephyr was stalking across the courtyard past other students to her right. Antheia was going up the steps to the Academy to her left. For half a second she wasn't sure who to follow, but then she went after Zephyr.

When she caught up to him, he just stood there, arms folded. "I thought the secret crush notescrolls were from you," he said flatly.

"Really?" Even though he was obviously mad, delight shot through her that he'd actually come to the grove to see *her. Not* Antheia. "How'd you know?"

He gave a snort. "Not hard to figure out. They were written and decorated with multicolored pens. I saw your writing in Ms. Hydra's sign-in book yesterday in

Zeus's office, remember? And then you gave me one of your pens to sign my name."

"Yeah." It was getting hard to see his face. Iris squinted, then looked up at the sky, which was now several shades darker than it had been even minutes before.

"Oh no!" she murmured in a terrified voice. His gaze followed hers to the enormous, dark gray tornado that was swirling around in the distance. It was headed their way.

"Godsamighty!" said Zephyr. "It's Typhon. He's coming!"

10

Terrible Typhon

Zephyr ushered Iris over to MOA's front steps. "Go. It'll be safer inside. I'll come back when I can. I have to find my brothers so we can fight this monster! We must protect Zeus at all costs!" Then he took off into the air, winds swirling.

"Wait! I saw Principal Zeus riding away on Pegasus a few hours ago!" she called to him, but Zephyr didn't hear over the roar of Typhon's approaching winds. The giant tornado filled the sky now, heading right for MOA. Upon seeing it approaching, everyone in the courtyard ran for cover.

Iris rushed to the top of the granite steps. But she *didn't* go inside, as all the other students had done. She needed to do something to help fight the monster. Only, what could she do? Her hair whipped across her face as she looked around wildly. The linen drape that the sculptor had left covering the completed anemometer in the courtyard blew off right then in a gust of wind that was far fiercer than the winds of Zephyr and his brothers. The anemometer began spinning around like a top, its cups a complete blur!

She pinned her arms to her sides to keep her chiton from flying up over her head. This was just all so horrible! Typhon was almost upon them, having finally made his move. And it seemed that MOA was completely unprepared. No one knew where Zeus was, and the four winds had been caught off guard too.

Zeus had said Typhon wasn't all that bright, and Iris couldn't help wondering if Gaia was the one behind this plan. Had the goddess told her son to lurk nearby awhile, doing nothing? Had the two of them been hoping this would throw Zeus off so that Typhon could take the Academy by surprise? If so, the ploy had worked! Except for one teeny thing. They must have thought Zeus was still at MOA, since he was the one Typhon really wanted to destroy above all else.

By now the entire sky looked like swirling, thick gray cotton candy. Iris gazed up at her beloved Mount Olympus Academy. Its usually sparkling white marble walls looked dull in the gloom that hung over every-thing. For a girl who was all about color, seeing the world around her turn so dark and dreary in the middle of the day was awful. Not to mention that she was worried about all of her friends.

Within minutes the tornado monster touched down at the far edge of the courtyard. "ME HAVE COME!" rumbled a deep, powerful voice. Iris pressed back against the Academy's big bronze doors as the words blasted out at her.

Now that Typhon had landed and stopped whirling, she could see him more clearly. He stood there, so tall that the clouds crowned his head. His whole body was covered with black feathers, and he had dozens of long thin, curly legs.

"ME HERE!" he bellowed, beating his chest. "AND ME SCARY!"

Huh? Typhon had very poor grammar, thought Iris. Was Zeus right about the monster? He certainly didn't *sound* very bright. Maybe they could use that against him somehow.

As he skittered closer, she heard hissing sounds. Then she saw that all those legs were actually gigantic serpent tails that coiled and uncoiled as he traveled. And his fingers were tipped with dragon heads that breathed real fire! Though he'd stopped whirling, strong winds still whipped around him, ripping up the torches that ringed the courtyard, and throwing them up into the air like giant batons.

By now the anemometer was spinning so fast, it seemed it would fly apart at any moment. Iris wrapped her arms around one of the tall Ionic columns in front of the school to keep from being blown away.

Suddenly Artemis and a group of godboys burst from the doors behind her and rushed down the school steps into the courtyard. Apollo and Artemis carried their bows and arrows. Ares held his spear. Poseidon had his trident. But they and their weapons looked puny and useless compared to the ginormous Typhon!

Bravely Artemis and Apollo notched arrows and drew back their bows. *Zing! Zing!* Their arrows bounced off Typhon like toothpicks. Poseidon and Ares had no better luck with their weapons.

"HEH, HEH, HEH!" Typhon laughed at them. Their efforts must seem pathetic to him! Fire flashed from his dragon fingers and his eyes, striking fear into the Olympians. His attackers scattered, looking for safety.

Then he kneeled down on the Academy steps and spread his arms wide. Toward Iris. She froze, expecting the worst. But the crushing blow never came.

Instead Typhon hardly noticed her as he reached for the Academy building instead. His hands slid around it as if he would hug it to his chest. His face pushed through the bronze front doors. His dragon fingers went from window to window, peeking inside. He must be looking for Zeus!

Fear for her friends and all the students and teachers at MOA unfroze Iris. She took a step toward the monster. Someone had to do something to stop him!

"He's not here!" she yelled.

Typhon didn't hear. Before she could shout again, the monster suddenly howled and lurched upright, whipping around. Zeus had flown in from behind him, riding on Pegasus! He was hurling thunderbolts at Typhon's back. *Zap! Zap!*

Hooray! thought Iris. But would even Zeus be a match for this terrible monster?

"OW! OW!" yelled Typhon. He fell backward, his coiled legs knocking over several statues as he tumbled down the steps. He was soon on his feet—er, serpent tails—again, however.

And he began to fight back. Uncoiling his tails, he struck Zeus with a mighty blow that sent him and

Pegasus spiraling through the air. They quickly recovered, and Zeus hit Typhon with another thunderbolt.

"OW!" yelled Typhon.

Just then Zeus spotted Iris and yelled something to her. But his words were lost in the ferocious winds.

"What?" Iris yelled back, cupping a hand around her ear. But he was already off again. He and his mighty winged horse flew this way and that, dodging serpentine tails as the monster lumbered after them. Zeus was methodically leading Typhon away from the Academy!

What had he yelled to her a minute ago? Pincher? Or picture? No! He must've said "pitcher"! Iris gasped. He wanted her to get Styx's *pitcher.* She was sure of it! Although she didn't know why he wanted it, at least it gave her something to do. A way to help. Was it in his office? She hoped so. She flung open the bronze doors and raced into the Academy.

Inside, students were running up and down the stairs and halls calling to each other as they searched for friends to make sure they were all safe for the moment. Ms. Hydra, Coach Triathlon, and some other teachers and students were barricading windows.

Mr. Cyclops, Professor Ladon (the Beast-ology teacher), Athena, and some of the godboys stood around a table they must have pulled from a classroom. They were bent over a map of the Academy with all its out-buildings and grounds. It looked like they were trying to formulate a battle plan to defend MOA against Typhon.

As Iris turned down the hall to Zeus's office, she passed Aphrodite and Persephone, who were helping to calm a crying student.

Then she ran into Antheia. "Thank godness! I've been looking for you," said her friend. Concern was etched on her face. "I saw you from a window a minute ago. I can't believe you were outside. Don't you know it's dangerous out there?"

"Tell me about it!" said Iris, barely slowing as Antheia fell into step beside her. "Zeus just arrived to fight Typhon. He told me to fetch a special pitcher that belongs to the Goddess Styx from his office. Help me find it?"

"I knew it!" said Pheme, overhearing as she fluttered up to them. "Zeus has a plan for defeating Typhon after all!" But then she frowned. "Only, how much help will a pitcher be? Hitting the monster over the head with it probably wouldn't do much good."

"I think he must have some other plan for it!" Iris called back as she ran.

Pheme paused, then flapped her wings and flitted the other way. Usually flying was banned in the hallways at school, but none of the teachers called her on it. This was an emergency! "I'll spread the word," she called back over her shoulder. "Everyone will take heart if Zeus has a plan—even if it's a lame one. And we could all use a bit of good news right now."

"Thanks!" Iris and Antheia kept running down the hall toward Zeus's office. Mere seconds after they got there, Athena, Aphrodite, and Medusa joined them to search for the pitcher too. Pheme was amazingly great at spreading the word in a crisis.

Quickly Iris described the pitcher to Antheia and Medusa, who'd never seen it. Then they all dove into the search. "We'll never find anything in this mess!" Medusa fretted at first. Then the snakes on her head pointed toward the desk.

"Good idea," said Aphrodite, and she and Medusa started rummaging through it.

"Why does my dad want the pitcher anyway?" Athena

asked breathlessly as she checked the shelves along the walls.

"Yeah. Like Pheme said, how is a pitcher going to help fight that gigantic beast?" Antheia wondered aloud, pawing through some stuff on a chair. She was trying to be brave, but her voice shook.

"I don't know," Iris admitted as she dug through a pile of things on the floor in a far corner of the office. All she came up with was a random sandal and a case of Zeus Juice. A few minutes later she and Antheia turned to the file cabinets. They yanked out drawers, and checked through them one by one.

"So, how long have you liked Zephyr?" Antheia asked out of the blue.

"What?" Iris said in surprise. They kept their voices low, so none of the others would overhear.

"I saw you talking to him in the courtyard after I

left the grove. And I could tell you were crushing. You should've told me."

At first Iris started to deny liking Zephyr, but then she remembered what Hera and Zeus had said about the advice the Gray Ladies' had given them. *Hmm,* she thought. Maybe that advice could apply to her situation too. Good communication was important between *any* two people, after all. And lying to her best friend about Zephyr, even it was to keep from hurting her, had *not* been good communication.

"You're right," Iris admitted. She tried to explain. "I was still sorting through my feelings when you said you liked Zephyr. So I backed off." Antheia's aura was a cool shade of indigo right now, so at least Iris's confession hadn't made her mad. Not yet, anyway.

Antheia tugged open another file cabinet drawer. Finding it full of maps, she shut it and tried a different drawer.

"The same thing happened with Poseidon and Apollo," Iris told her cautiously.

Antheia paused in her rifling of the file cabinet to send Iris a shocked look. "What? Are you kidding me? You liked *both of them* too? Wow, I didn't know." She fiddled with some lightning-bolt-shaped game pieces from a Thunderopoly game she'd just come across. Seeming to recall the urgency of their mission, she dropped them and went back to digging around for the pitcher.

A few seconds of silence passed before she added, "Or maybe I sort of did. The thing is, I never know which boys are crush-worthy. And I trust your opinion. So if you seem to like a boy okay, I figure he's a good choice."

Iris blinked. "So you go after him before I even have a chance to decide if I truly like him? Or if the boy might like me?"

Antheia looked stricken now. "I guess I do. *Did.* I'm sooo sorry!"

"It's okay. I know you didn't mean to—" Iris began. Suddenly her hand touched something smooth in the back of the last file cabinet drawer. She pulled out . . . the pitcher. "Found it!" she shouted gleefully. Without another word she jumped up and ran for the door. As she carried the pitcher down the hall to the front doors of the Academy, Antheia, Athena, Aphrodite, and Medusa were right alongside her.

The five of them burst out onto the front steps of MOA. High in the air across the courtyard, Typhon and the King of the Gods were still battling it out. And now the four winds were helping. But they and Zeus seemed no match for such a fearsome creature.

"Zeus is too far away for me to ask him what he wants me to do with this pitcher!" Iris moaned.

"Maybe we can figure it out ourselves," Athena said. "What do we know about it?"

"The pitcher? It looks old, for one thing," Medusa replied.

"And it acts like a lie detector when you drink from it," added Aphrodite.

"It does?" said Antheia and Medusa at the same time.

Iris nodded. "I drank from it, but then told the truth. So I don't know if it really works to catch a lie or not." When Antheia looked surprised at this announcement, Iris added, "I'll explain later."

"I wonder what would happen if someone drank from it and *did* lie?" Athena mused. "Its inscription says there are consequences, but—"

Iris gasped as she remembered again what Zeus had said about Typhon. That the monster was not very bright. Suddenly she had an idea of why Zeus might've asked her to find the pitcher.

"That's it!" she said. While holding the pitcher tightly under one arm, she formed a ball of magic in her opposite hand, drew back, and pitched the ball skyward. *Brrrng!* Dazzling colors rushed from her fingertips, sailed in a high arc past Typhon's nose, and then shot downward to end far beyond the courtyard.

"Wow!" said Antheia. The other girls murmured their amazement too. The rainbow looked more vibrant and strong than any Iris had created before!

Even Typhon seemed mesmerized by it. He'd stopped in his tracks to stare.

"What's wrong with him?" Medusa wondered aloud.

"I think he's fascinated by Iris's rainbow. He's probably never seen anything so colorful," said Antheia.

"Right. He's been trapped in Tartarus since the end

of our war with the Titans," said Athena. When Medusa looked blank, she added, "Mr. Cyclops, Hero-ology."

"Oh, yeah," said Medusa, who sometimes seemed to spend more class time painting her fingernails green than studying.

Appearing delighted by the colors Iris had created, Typhon had faltered in his fighting. But maybe not for long. Without giving herself a chance to chicken out, Iris leaped atop the rainbow she'd made. The other girls gasped in surprise as she slid upward along its slope.

"What are you doing? Go back!" Zephyr called when he saw her gliding up the rainbow toward Typhon. He zoomed over to her and began to follow protectively alongside as she ascended, all the while keeping a wary eye on the monster.

Iris's hair, which was turning all sorts of colors one after the other, swirled and whirled around her in the wild winds. "No. I'm staying. You guys need my help. But just in case we're blown to smithereens by Typhon, I have to tell you I'm so sorry about what happened in the olive grove before."

"You want to talk about that *now*?" he asked.

She nodded, still concentrating on sliding smoothly upward. "We weren't making fun of you. Antheia really likes you. But she didn't know how to tell you, so she asked me to help her do it. I didn't really want to write those notes for her, or hide behind the tree and tell her stuff to say, but she's my bestie. So—"

"I came to the grove because I like *you*," interrupted Zephyr. "And I thought the notes meant you liked me back."

"I do!" she blurted. She put her fingers over her lips, wishing she could call her words back. Then she remembered about good communication and how it was, well, good.

And she was even gladder she'd told Zephyr the truth when his head whipped around to gaze at her. Because he looked rather . . . happy.

But for now Iris had a job to do. An important delivery to make. Only, first she had to get a certain monster's attention. "See you later," she told Zephyr firmly. Since the monster had started attacking again, Zephyr reluctantly left her side, returning to help his brothers fight.

"Hey, Typhon!" Iris called out as she reached the top of her rainbow.

"WHAH?" the beast boomed. Although he looked her way, his dragon fingers and coiled serpent legs still fought the four winds and Zeus. And it looked like Typhon was winning!

Iris held up the pitcher before the monster's fiery eyes. "See this pitcher?" she told him. "I need to deliver it to Zeus. It's his most prized possession, so please, I beg of you, let me take it to him. He would be hurt beyond all reason if you took it from me. He might even start crying."

She waited, hoping Zeus had heard her and would-confirm her statement. However, just then, one of Typhon's coiled legs knocked the King of the Gods far across the sky. Four of his other legs coiled around Boreas, Zephyr, Notus, and Eurus and squeezed them tight. With his enemies held captive for the moment, Typhon reached out two dragon fingers and snatched the pitcher from Iris, just as she'd hoped he would. In his ginormous hand it looked like a thimble with a tiny handle!

"Oh no! I can't believe you did that, you . . . you horrible monster!" Iris wailed, pretending to be upset.

Typhon grinned as if she'd just given him the best compliment ever.

Encouraged, she went on, "Please, please, I beg of

you, give it back!" she called to him in a faked, worried tone. "The water inside is precious to Zeus. He would be totally devastated if you drank it."

"HEH! HEH!" Typhon laughed his loud, dark laugh. Then he pulled out the round stopper, carelessly tossed it over his shoulder, and lifted the pitcher to his mouth. He swallowed the water inside the pitcher—which was no more than a drop to him—in one gulp.

"Oh no! I can't believe you did that too!" Iris cried out again. "When I visited the Goddess Styx this morning, she told me you were too dumb to think for yourself. And she said it was Gaia's idea for you to fight Zeus and that without your mommy's—that is, Gaia's—help you'd still be stuck in Tartarus."

"WHAH?" roared Typhon "HER WRONG!" With each word he spoke, there came a flash of lightning. Somewhere within the dark swirling clouds, Zeus was still fighting the monster, tossing thunderbolts right and left. But they were like sparky toothpicks to Typhon. He was that huge!

"Really?" Iris said, faking surprise. "I guess Styx was lying, then." She paused, wanting to phrase what she said next very, very carefully. "So," she said at last, "does that mean that you escaped Tartarus on your own? And that it was your idea—and your idea alone—to come here to fight Zeus?" She held her breath as she awaited his reply.

Typhon stopped thrashing the four godboys with his snaky limbs as he considered her question. If she could have seen an aura around him, she might have been able to guess how he would answer. But he was a completely colorless character. No aura whatsoever.

"Well," she prompted him. "Are you and Gaia working together?"

A shifty look came into his eyes. "NO. ME NOT IN

CAHOOTS WITH MY MOMMY. ME OWN BOSS. ME ESCAPE TARTARUS BY MYSELF. AND ME THINK OF IDEA TO BEAT ZEUS."

A smile tugged at Iris's lips. Because she was pretty sure she'd just caught him in a big fat lie! Would it do the job? She waited to see what would happen, and she didn't have to wait long.

"UGH, ME DIZZY," Typhon suddenly complained. He dropped Zeus and the four winds pronto and put a dragon-fingered hand to his forehead. The air began to whoosh like crazy as he began turning around and around, spinning faster and faster until he became a blur. He'd turned into a tornado again!

If Iris had been perched upon a less sturdy rainbow, she surely would have been blown away. But her rainbow held, and her feet stayed firmly planted upon it.

Meanwhile the Typhon tornado began to shrink,

coiling smaller . . . and smaller . . . and smaller, until he was the size of a whirlpool in a bathtub. One end of the whirling tornado funneled itself into the pitcher, which was still held aloft on his winds. With a tremendous slurping, sucking sound like water going down a drain, the rest of the tiny, whirly gray monster followed, corkscrewing itself all the way inside. Then it disappeared. Captured! Instantly the air went still.

The pitcher began to fall toward the ground. If it broke, Typhon would escape!

"No!" Iris called out. As the pitcher sailed downward, it passed a half-dozen feet from her. She made a wild dive for it. Her fingers grabbed the pitcher's handle, and she covered its opening with the flat of her other hand. "Gotcha now, monster!" she cried out, hugging the pitcher close. But now that she'd jumped off the rainbow, she began hurtling downward as well.

She couldn't create another rainbow to land on while holding the pitcher with both hands. Yet she couldn't very well drop the pitcher and set Typhon free again. But then again, the pitcher—and she—would break on impact. What was she going to do?

Oomph! Just a few dozen feet above the courtyard, she landed on a soft, springy cushion of air. Zephyr winged over, still blowing hard to create the winds she now rested upon, his cheeks puffed and round. He'd saved her!

She nodded toward the pitcher she'd managed to hang on to. "Where's its stopper?" she called to him.

"Here!" Boreas shouted, flying it over with Notus and Eurus. "I caught it when Typhon tossed it away. Let's seal that pitcher once and for all." To her surprise the annoying boy was acting serious now and really trying to be helpful. Was it possible Mr. Frosty-Pants had a good side?

As Iris stuck the stopper into the top of the pitcher,

sealing Typhon's doom, Zeus soared toward her and the four winds on Pegasus. "Good work! I'll take that."

Iris gladly gave him the pitcher while the windy godboys gathered around. "What will you do with Typhon this time?" she asked.

Zeus stared at the pitcher for a second, pondering Typhon's fate. "I guess even Tartarus wasn't strong enough to hold this guy," he finally replied. "Especially since Gaia knew he was there. So I'll take him to a secret place he'll never escape from and where his rumbling won't even be noticed. A volcano, whose location I won't reveal to anyone."

With that, he and Pegasus took off for the secret location of the volcano and quickly disappeared into the distance. And just like that, the clouds of Typhon's rampage gave way to clear, sunny skies.

11

Iris of the Rainbows

ALL WAS PEACEFUL AT THE ACADEMY THE NEXT day. The sky dawned a bright blue with puffy white clouds and a sunrise that looked tickled pink to Iris. Zeus had deposited Typhon in the depths of the volcano somewhere and returned sometime during the night.

After breakfast he summoned all MOA students to the courtyard, where they gathered for a dedication ceremony to unveil the new anemometer. It still sat in the courtyard amid the rubble left from Typhon's attack, and the linen drape now covered it again.

Zeus stood at a podium halfway up MOA's granite steps. First off he called the anemometer's creator, Pygmalion, up to give a short speech.

"I am the greatest sculptor who has ever lived, and this is the greatest anemometer ever created in the history of the world," the sculptor declared bluntly. "I hope it proves useful, Olympians. Please enjoy it." Then he gave a little bow and left the podium.

"Still so humble," Iris heard Aphrodite say from somewhere behind her. There was a teasing smile in her voice. Back when Aphrodite and the Egyptian goddess Isis had argued about which of them was the real goddess of love, Pygmalion had helped judge the outcome. He was rumored to have acted quite pompously, and it seemed obvious that he still thought very highly of himself.

“And now . . . miraculously unharmed by Typhon . . .” In a dramatic move Zeus whipped off the huge sheet of linen that covered the statue. “The new MOA anemometer!”

Gasps and cheers sounded throughout the crowd. As Iris studied the device again, which she’d never really had a chance to do before, with Typhon attacking and all, she had to admit that Pygmalion was pretty much right about the awesomeness of his talent. The anemometer was amazing! And he’d sculpted it in record time.

About ten feet tall, its main post was labeled *N*, *S*, *E*, and *W* for the different directions. And a life-size sculpture of a different windy godboy had been carved on each of the four sides of the post. Their cheeks were puffed out as if they were blowing out the swirls of wind that Pygmalion had sculpted around them. As the device turned, the figures of the wind-brothers did as well. So each got a chance to face prominently forward at one time or another, and no one of them appeared more important than another. *Nice work, Pygmalion,* thought Iris.

There were oohs and aahs as everyone admired the anemometer. Then Zeus spoke again, calling the four gods of wind to the podium. "I want to thank Boreas, Zephyr, Notus, and Eurus for their help in defeating Typhon. This anemometer will always serve as a reminder of their prowess in battle and their dedication to Olympian might and right. They will be leaving us soon, but they are welcome back at MOA anytime."

Everyone clapped and cheered as each godboy spoke briefly. "My brothers and I fought well," Boreas declared, being generous with credit for once. "Though I think I deserve—"

"Ahem!" Zeus interrupted. A warning perhaps that he'd said enough? Taking the hint, Boreas broke off.

There was an awkward pause as he took his place beside his brothers again.

Then Zephyr punched his fist into the air. "Hooray for blowhards!" Which made the audience laugh and cheer some more. The four godboys high-fived, then left the podium.

After that the crowd began to break up. Lots of students crowded around the four windy brothers. But almost immediately Zephyr came over to Iris and drew her aside. "So we never finished talking before. And I'm wondering if you're going to let Antheia stand in the way of liking me?"

"Well, it's just that she liked you *first*," said Iris. "Or at least she said so first. And I don't steal crushes from my BFF."

"I admire that kind of friend loyalty. But I'm never going to crush on Antheia," Zephyr told her. "Because it's you I like."

A warm feeling flooded through her at his words. Then something beyond her seemed to catch his attention. "Hmm. Maybe that whole Antheia thing's not going to be a problem anymore," he said.

Iris turned to see that Aphrodite was walking with Antheia, sort of herding her toward where Boreas was standing. The three of them began talking. Then Aphrodite slipped off, leaving the two alone. Antheia's and Boreas's heads were soon together, and they were chatting and laughing away about something.

Iris could hardly believe it. She'd guessed that Boreas liked her friend, and she'd been wondering if she should steer Antheia in his direction, in spite of his boastful, bullying ways. And now she didn't have to decide. Aphrodite had done the matchmaking for her. Three cheers for the goddessgirl of love!

Somehow Aphrodite must've figured out that

Antheia and Boreas were meant for each other before they'd figured it out themselves. Which made Iris feel confident that even though she had reservations about Boreas, he'd turn out to be perfect for her friend. She had a happy feeling that Antheia's affections were about to make another switch.

She looked at Zephyr to find him studying her, and smiled at him. "I think you could be right."

"You! Ibis," Zeus called out suddenly, making Iris jump. She turned to see that he was at the podium again. Hera stood beside him, looking expectant.

"Ibis?" Zephyr echoed, grinning.

Iris rolled her eyes, grinning back. "The King of the Gods is not so good with names."

"Up here. Now!" Zeus boomed at her. Every eye swung her way, and she hunched down a little.

"What did I do now?" she wondered aloud.

"Go on!" Athena urged her. She, Aphrodite, Artemis, Antheia, and Persephone had come over. Now they shooed her toward the steps. As Iris went, students gathered around the podium again to see what was going to happen.

"I forgot to congratulate the most important person of all in the fight against Typhon," Zeus announced when she was finally standing by his side. "Her name is . . ."

"It's Iris," she told him quickly.

"Of course it is. I knew that," Zeus replied. Then to the crowd he boomed, "Her name is Iris!"

Then he turned to her, speaking loudly enough that everyone would hear. "I'm pleased with what you did to defeat Typhon. Your quick thinking and decisive action are what saved us in the end, and we are all grateful. So I—"

Just then the anemometer began to whirl. The wind had picked up. And at the back of the crowd there was a loud thump. Oh no! Had Typhon somehow escaped? Was he back? Wariness swept those gathered around as everyone swiveled to look.

But it was only the Hermes' Delivery Service chariot landing at the back of the courtyard. *Phew!* thought Iris. The crowd parted for Hermes, who stomped through to deliver an armload of packages. He dumped them onto the school steps and then stomped up to the podium.

"You look terrible," Zeus told him frankly.

"I *feel* terrible," Hermes said grumpily. "I'm exhausted. I need help. An assistant. Now."

"I see," said Zeus, stroking his red beard thoughtfully.

Hera set a hand on Iris's shoulder, a slow smile crossing her face. "How about Iris?" she suggested to Zeus.

Iris perked up. "Yeah. I could help you, Hermes,"

she volunteered. This was just what she'd been hoping for. A worthwhile job she knew she could do if given the chance. "You could train me to deliver messages in my spare time, like an extracurricular."

Zeus smiled, appearing to like the idea. Unfortunately, Hermes didn't.

"A *student* helper?" he grumped. "Your wings don't look very strong. They'll probably give out on a long-distance delivery."

Iris knew she had to do something really impressive right away, or she might lose this opportunity. "I don't need my wings. I've got something better. Watch this!" she said. Quickly she wound up and threw a ball of magic from the courtyard to the top of MOA. *Brrrng!*

When a rainbow appeared, she slid up it to the roof and back down to the podium again within seconds. "See?" she said breathlessly. "I can use my rainbows to slide to Earth and distant lands to deliver messages and packages for you."

"Not bad," Hermes said, a new respect in his voice. "So you're the goddessgirl of rainbows, then?"

"Well, not officially." She glanced at Zeus.

"What's everyone looking at?" he said, appearing perplexed. But then Hera gently nudged him in the side and whispered something into his ear.

"Oh," he said. "I see." He turned toward the crowd and spread his arms wide. "I just got a great idea!" he boomed to all assembled. "In honor of Iris's heroism, I hereby officially appoint her the Goddess of Rainbows!"

"Wow! Really? How cool is that?" Pheme practically yelled from the back of the crowd. Then she was off to Earth to spread the news. "It's official. Iris is the goddessgirl of rainbows!"

Zeus beamed at Iris. "Good work. You deserve this honor."

She left the podium a few minutes later, feeling as though she were floating on air, even though there wasn't any wind blowing. At the bottom of the steps, she and Antheia did an impromptu happy dance. Then Athena, Artemis, Aphrodite, and Persephone enveloped them both in a group hug. It seemed that everyone wanted to congratulate her.

When Zephyr drew near, her friends melted away. "Now that Typhon's been defeated, it's time for me and my brothers to go," he told her.

"Oh," said Iris. She heard the disappointment in her own voice.

"But we'll be back," Boreas assured her. And his frosty smile actually warmed when he glanced at Antheia, who was standing nearby.

"Yeah! You can't stop the wind!" said Notus and Eurus.

As all four brothers lifted off, Zephyr waved farewell to Iris. "See you soon!" he called to her. She waved back. Then the winds whirled away, each in a different direction. Boreas to the north, Zephyr to the west, Notus to the south, and Eurus to the east.

"So you like Boreas?" Iris asked Antheia once the four brothers were gone.

Antheia nodded, smiling sweetly. "Yeah, I kind of do. We have a lot in common, actually. Turns out he loves wreaths." She paused before adding, "Well, he loves blowing them around, anyway."

Iris laughed. Then Antheia turned serious. "I thought about what you said about crush stealing."

"Oh?" Iris said lightly.

Antheia nodded. "Let's promise that we'll always be

friends, and that we'll always be honest about who we like from now on, okay?"

A slow smile spread across Iris's face, and she nodded. "To friendship! And to boys never, ever, ever coming between us again."

"Pact," they said at the same time. Both girls hooked pinky fingers to make it binding. Then they giggled, and the newly anointed goddessgirl of rainbows and her best friend, the goddess of wreaths, headed up the stairs to Mount Olympus Academy together.

Don't miss the next adventure in the Goddess Girls series!

Coming Soon